IMMORTAL TRUTHS

AN ANGEL AND HER DEMONS: BOOK TWO

LACEY CARTER ANDERSEN

DEDICATION

To my readers—thank you for reading my stories.

~ Lacey Carter Andersen

CONNECT WITH LACEY

Want to be part of the writing process? Maybe even get a taste of my sense of humor? Teasers for my new releases? And more?

1

M *any years ago...*

MARK WAS JUST a boy when he came upon the forbidden waters in the sanctuary. The small pond, surrounded by a garden imbued with druid magic, was only for the Immortals to bathe within. Every druid knew that, from the time they could walk. And yet, he was drawn to this place. He always had been.

Mark stared into the simple pool, transfixed. When he set his staff down in the greenery, the plants rose from where they lay, curling around him like favorite pets. They tangled in greeting with the plants that grew upon his brown robe. Mark smiled and stroked the green leaves, reassuring them.

I'm not here to cause trouble.

The elders were busy, and for the first time since he

could remember, no one was in this sacred place. *I can finally get close enough to investigate.*

He had no intention of touching the waters. Touching them meant death to any but the Immortals. He only wanted to look, to see why they called to him.

He told his father once that magic pulled him to it, that he had dreams of the water calling his name.

His father had placed a strong hand on his shoulder. "Druids are rare and precious things. There are few of us left. You are the only child to be born from your generation, and you will one day be responsible for protecting this sacred place and for leading your people."

"But the waters—"

"Are not calling to you." His father's words left no room for arguments. "We druids do not interfere with the destiny of the world. We are here only to keep this place safe."

"But why? You said the Immortals are long gone, and that Caine will rule forever. So if this place has no destiny, and we have no role to play in all of it, why does this place still exist? Why do we protect it?"

His father smiled, one of his rare smiles, and rubbed his son's head. "My son, always so full of questions and curiosity. You make your father very proud."

He smiled up at the man he worshipped with everything in him. The man who was all the family he had after his mother's death. "And the answers to my questions?"

The old druid knelt down. "We keep this place sacred because it's our role. It has always been our role. The long dead Immortals change none of that. We are one of only a handful of beings that remember a time before him—a time before he wiped the world of its memories. And so, we must remain here, and remember, but we take no action. Do you understand?"

He didn't understand. What did it all matter if they kept this place safe for nothing? If they used their powers for nothing? What was the point in weaving their magic into sacred lands that Caine and his followers could never reach, if they had no one to protect?

But his father rose, and walked away, leaving him with troubling thoughts. He knew as a druid his job was to obey, and yet, even then, the waters called to him. They whispered of a destiny not yet fulfilled. And yet, he didn't understand.

So now, with the elders finally busy, he knelt before the waters, hoping the sacred liquid would finally answer his questions. His fingers ached to touch the waters, to skim his fingertips across the top. Instead, he curled his fingers into his palm and stretched his senses out, feeling the power humming from his staff beside him, warming him.

He stared and stared. And yet, nothing happened. Nothing changed.

I guess my dreams of Immortals and destiny are nothing but that... dreams.

Grasping the handle on his staff, he rose. But to his horror, the top of his staff brushed the waters.

Heart beating fast, he looked between where the liquid slid down the dark wood of his most sacred item. Would the waters destroy it?

Beneath him, the pool began to bubble.

He took a step back, watching with wide eyes as the bubbles rose sharply, and then collapsed, leaving the water absolutely still.

A woman's face appeared in the pool. Her hair was golden, and it flowed down her bare shoulders. Her eyes were strange... so powerful that they seemed to call to him.

"I am Atropos, the Fate of the past. And you, young druid, are going to change the world."

He couldn't speak, nor could he move. He simply stood, rooted in place, staring down at the face of a powerful being.

"Your role will not be easy, little one. In fact, we place a great deal on your shoulders. But believe me, it's necessary. You're the only one who can do it."

"What?" he whispered, the word slipping past his lips.

"You will take our gift, and you will learn how to use it. And when the time is right, you shall find the Immortals and overthrow Caine."

He inched closer to her. For some reason, he wasn't afraid. Her words rang true down to his very soul. This is what the water had wanted from him all along. This is what his dreams had meant.

Her beautiful face curled into the saddest smile. "I'm sorry for the heartbreak this will cause. I'm sorry for how you will suffer. But Lachey, my sister, told me, long before her disappearance, that you will be rewarded in the end with the most precious thing in this world: love."

Mark stared, unsure what to say.

"I'm sorry," she whispered.

The waters rose up like a hand and grasped him, dragging him down. He was trapped beneath the water, struggling for his life. For the first time, he knew real terror as bubbles of air left his mouth.

But there, before him, a necklace lifted up from the waters. It glowed softly, with an ancient magic. And the stone in the center glistened. It moved to encircle his neck, dropping onto him with a weight that surprised him.

He expected to escape the waters then, but he remained. Struggling, drowning, in fear for his life, until everything went black.

When he awoke, his people stood around him, the boy

soaking wet beside a pool destined for Immortals. The pool would have killed any other creature, yet he was alive.

He tried to tell them, to show them, but none of them could see the necklace. He spoke of the Fate and his role in the future. He tried to convince them of what he knew.

The people drew away from him in fear, but he couldn't stop sharing the message from the Fate. Days passed. Weeks passed.

At last, he was brought before the elders, before his father, to learn his fate.

They'd determined that he'd lost his mind. That he'd never fallen into the sacred waters. That he had no necklace, and no destiny.

And that he also no longer had a place amongst them.

When his father took Mark's staff, Mark didn't know what to expect. A staff was like a druid's soul, carved for them at their birth. It grew as they grew, and it became more powerful as they did.

So as he stared at his father with the innocent eyes of a child, he didn't know what to expect. When his father cracked his staff over his leg, the sound echoed through his very soul. He screamed and collapsed onto his knees, clawing at his chest until blood ran down his flesh.

When he lay upon the ground, scared in a way that no one could ever understand, the elders lifted him, while his father explained his exile. They carried him out of the sacred sanctuary, beyond the barrier that safeguarded their protected lands, and they dumped him beside a road.

None of them looked back as he called their names and wept.

Instead, he was a child alone in a world he didn't understand, with the weight of the world around his neck.

Right then, he didn't think about how he would find the Immortals or how he would defeat Caine. He only cried and begged for his father. Because even with such responsibility, he was just a boy.

2

Surcy stretched out her arms and legs, feeling the sun on her face and the wind in her hair. Her hands reached out further and further. For one glorious moment, she felt like she was flying. She even imagined her wings stretching out behind her. And it was... beautiful. Perfect.

But those aren't my wings. Just hard concrete.

Her eyes opened, and she felt the building beneath her back. Of course she wasn't flying. She was an angel with no wings.

Tears tracked down her cheeks. Lying on the roof was the closest that she came to feeling like an angel again. And it was just pathetic.

Why can't I stop? Why can't I just accept that I'll never be the same again?

A tingle ran down her spine. Her gaze moved and connected with Tristan's. He sat on the edge of their home like he was truly a gargoyle, made of stone, even in his human form. His mismatched eyes held a wealth of emotion for one painful moment, before he closed them. When he opened them once more, he was devoid of all emotion.

Gargoyles are far too good at hiding the way they feel.

And too quiet.

"What are you doing here?" she asked, wiping away her tears.

He rose out of his crouch, still standing on the edge of the building. In the early morning sun, he was like a god. He was tall and muscular, huge in a way that only a gargoyle or a demon could be. His long dark hair hung loosely around his shoulders, and his stance was that of a protector.

A quiver ran through her body. She wanted this man, even though he was a demon. And yet, neither Tristan nor Mark would touch her yet. She wasn't sure if they were waiting to see if her memories would return, or if they were still worried that she was too fragile, but it drove her mad.

He leapt down from the edge of the building and came close to her, until his shadow blocked out the sun. "If you would like, I can take you flying."

His words hurt something deep inside her. She didn't want him to take her into the sky. She wanted her own wings.

"No, thanks."

He cocked his head. "You miss it. You lay up here each morning pretending to fly. Why not let me help?"

It took her a second to answer. "It's not the same."

He nodded, then knelt down beside her. "What can I do for you?"

Her throat went dry. When she and Daniel fucked, she felt... alive for a little while, but the feeling didn't last. She didn't understand why. He'd told her that it had changed her in some profound way before, and she wanted that now more than anything. If she couldn't be an angel, she needed to be human again. *Something real.*

Leaning up, she ran her fingers through his hair.

His eyes widened, and he stood frozen while she touched him. His hair. His jaw. At last, she pulled him slowly down to her and kissed him.

He groaned, and suddenly, he was kissing her back, desperately, his mouth hard and confident.

When she parted her lips, he rose over her and lay down on top of her. Then, his tongue moved into her mouth.

She moaned, rubbing herself against his hard erection.

He broke their kiss.

She stared up at him, panting. "Please?"

His eyes closed, his jaw locked. "Surcy…"

She slid her hands under his shirt, stroking the hard muscles of his stomach. Then, trailing her hands down, she gripped his cock through his pants.

His eyes flashed open. "Do you love me?"

She tensed.

"Do you?" he asked again.

Her heart hammered. "Tristan, I—"

"You still don't remember me. You still don't care for me like that."

Her hand dropped. "Can't we just pretend for a little while?"

"You might be able to, but I can't." The misery in his gaze was heart wrenching.

"I want to remember. You know that, right?"

He nodded, then rolled off of her.

Standing, he turned his strong back to her, hands clenched.

"I'm sorry," she whispered.

She wasn't sure he'd heard her when his gruff voice came. "Mark wants to talk to us."

"Okay."

The gargoyle moved to the edge of the building and leapt off, drifting above the tall trees that surrounded their home. She stared after him, hating the emotions coursing through her. There was nothing she could do to right things between them. It seemed they were tortured both by her touch and by her lack of touch.

So, I guess we'll just keep pretending.

Rising, she hurried down the stairs that led to the rooftop and walked down the long hallway that had doors leading to each of their rooms. At the end of it, she stepped out into the large living room. Her gaze immediately went to the back wall of massive glass doors and the incredible garden Mark had planted around their home. It grew wild and beautiful, transforming the simple room into something extraordinary.

When she was alone, the view was almost soothing. But in moments like this, it was like something incredible... that she wasn't a part of.

But apparently I helped plant it. If only I remembered. She turned her gaze away from it, hating how everything seemed to be triggering her sadness.

I need to snap out of this!

A movement drew her gaze. Mark sat quietly on the couch in the living room, and her heart clenched. He must have been using the God Finder again. The circles under his eyes were darker than ever, and he looked pale.

For a moment, she stood in the doorway, her gaze transfixed by him. Mark was a good-looking man. He wasn't as broad as Tristan, but he was taller, with tight muscles that bulged beneath his collared shirts.

When he turned to her, his mouth twisted into a tired smile. "Did you sleep well?"

She'd been having nightmares about Caine lately, but when she woke up, they slipped away like shadows.

"About the same," she said, walking across the room and sitting in the overly-large chair near the cold fireplace.

"I'll make you some tea tonight."

She smiled. "Maybe you need to make some tea for yourself too."

He winced. "Do I look that bad?"

"Never," she laughed. "But you do look like you need a good night's sleep."

He stroked the chain on his ancient necklace, The God Finder, and looked troubled. "I couldn't sleep until I knew for sure... and now I do."

"Knew?" she asked, sitting up straighter. *Has he discovered another Immortal?*

"Morning!"

Every muscle in her body tensed. Turning, she tried not to stare at Daniel, but he looked so damn good. His normally perfectly styled blond hair was still messy from sleep, and all he wore was a pair of dark boxers.

Her mouth watered. It'd been a couple days since she'd touched him last. If Mark wasn't in the room, she wouldn't have been able to control herself. Her hands twitched, wanting to touch his massive biceps, wanting to lick her way down his chest and belly.

"You look hungry," he told her, and she didn't miss the sexual innuendo behind his words. "How about we all sit at the table and have some coffee?"

Mark rubbed his face. "I could actually use some coffee."

She and Mark moved to the little table, and Daniel

poured them all a cup of coffee, and an additional one in front of Tristan's spot.

Then, Daniel scooted his chair closer to her, smirked, and sipped his coffee. She and Mark added lots of cream and sugar, and then they were all drinking their coffee in silence.

"So, you said there was something you wanted to talk about," Daniel hedged, looking at the other demon.

Mark nodded, looking more tired by the minute. "But I wanted to wait for Tristan."

As if on cue, the gargoyle landed on the deck just outside the massive glass doors He folded his grey wings onto his back, before shifting. His wings disappeared, and his stone-colored skin turned to a human tan color in an instant. Then, he opened the doors and strode in. Without looking at her, he crossed the room and sat at the table beside them.

She took another sip of her coffee, waiting for whatever Mark had to say, when she felt Daniel's hand on her thigh. Tensing, it took all her effort to swallow the liquid in her mouth.

Daniel's hands stroked the sensitive skin of her thigh, just below her small pajama shorts. Every muscle in her body tensed, and her core heated up. She wanted his touch more than anything in this world. But at breakfast? In front of the others?

We couldn't. Could we?

His fingers slipped beneath her shorts and into her underwear.

She was breathing hard as he stroked her mound, not yet entering her.

"I found another Immortal," Mark said.

Her gaze snapped to him, but she was intimately aware of the fire mage's fingers stroking her slowly.

"Where?" Tristan asked.

"I can't say for sure, but I know enough to be able to show Surcy where to go."

Daniel parted her folds and started to stroke her there, sliding along her wet body. He avoided her clit, just circled and circled it, driving her wild. She spread her legs wider and set her coffee down, gripping the edge of the table.

"Do we know what kind of Immortal it is?" Daniel asked, and she hated how normal he sounded.

She could barely hear Mark's response over her panting. "Some kind of shifter god. The images that keep flashing in my mind don't... they don't make sense, but I'm thinking I might understand them when we get there."

Daniel ran a soft finger over her clit, and she bit down a moan. Then, his finger continued on, sliding into her.

She was going to lose her mind. She wanted to buck against him. To ride him. But she knew Mark and Tristan couldn't find out what they were doing. If they did, all hell would break loose.

"So what's the plan?" Daniel asked, and she swore there was a husky quality to his voice.

She bit down on a string of curses when he added a second finger to the first and began to slowly plunge in and out of her. Every muscle in her body twitched and squeezed, needing more. Needing release.

Mark adjusted his glasses and drained the rest of his coffee, before setting it down. "I need Tristan's help with a few things, but then we should teleport right there. Maybe this afternoon?"

She nodded, swallowing down her building desire. "Sounds like... a plan."

Daniel pulled his fingers free, then squeezed her clit while she dug her nails into the edge of the table. "Surcy and I will get ready then."

Mark nodded and rose.

Daniel put her underwear back into place and finished his coffee.

She stayed sitting, her legs trembling. She waited until Mark and Tristan left through the front door before she was able to breathe.

With Mark and Tristan gone, she turned to Daniel. "That was a dick move."

In response, he stood, his massive erection right in front of her face. "Want to even the score?"

Damn it. She should tell him no, but she was already reaching for him. Stroking his head through his dark boxers, she loved that precum already coated the material. Pushing the boxers to the side, she pulled him out of one side and leaned forward, taking his tip into her mouth.

His hand dug into the back of her hair and he pulled her onto her knees, forcing himself deeper. Her arousal roared like a fire as he began to fuck her mouth like a man desperate for release.

When he looked on the edge of exploding, he froze, his eyes opening. "You feel so fucking good, you know that?"

Reaching out, he tugged down her shirt. Her braless breasts came out of the top of her tanktop and he swore, pinching the tips. She gasped, and he shoved his dick deeper into her mouth. She gagged around him, and his grip on her nipples grew harder.

"You like it when I fuck you like this don't you?"

She nodded.

"You like taking my cock deep?" He pulled himself out of her mouth.

It took her a second to answer. "Yes."

He took his shaft and moved it between her breasts, grasping her mounds and pulling them around him. "You want me to fuck your breasts?"

"Yes," she moaned.

"I want you to touch yourself when I do it."

She nodded, sliding one hand into her underwear. She wasn't surprised to find herself wet, and sensitive, every stroke of her fingers sent desire shooting through her.

And all the while, he slammed his cock between her breasts like a declaration.

"I own you," he groaned. "Say it."

"You own me," she panted.

"Open your mouth."

She did. Every time he slid between her breasts, his tip entered her mouth. She stroked herself harder and harder, aching for release. Aching for him inside of her.

At last, he pulled back. Grabbing her arm, he yanked her into the kitchen. Pushing her over the counter, he tore her shorts and underwear off.

"Spread your legs."

She did.

He gripped her thighs and eased into her wet body from behind.

"Stroke your clit," he ordered.

She reached down and began to stroke herself, even though her muscles were twitching, as if overloaded.

His big cock pushed further, deeper, and she gasped. He was so big. But from behind... he was massive, filling her in a way that was almost painful.

When he came to his hilt, he kissed her back, and then, pulled out, before slamming back in. He rode her like a wild man while she chanted his name. His shaft sent her inner muscles tensing, squeezing, and the feeling was inde-scribable.

When she began to grind against her fingers and bounce against his dick, her orgasm came like a wave, and she couldn't stop. It felt so good. Too damn good.

Her vision went white, and she kept screaming his name, squeezing him as she rode the waves of her pleasure.

When he finally came, shouting her name, she swore his warm cum sent her over the edge once more. After several long moments of him plunging in and out, and her riding him like a wild animal, stretched beyond comfort, he fell on top of her.

For a long time, they stayed like that, with him still buried inside of her, breathing hard.

When he pulled out, he gave her ass a slap, and said. "You are one amazing lay. Now, better shower and get dressed."

He turned and walked away.

She rose up onto her elbows and watched him as he grabbed his boxers and disappeared into his room. She'd wanted this to be about just sex, and nothing else. She'd wanted a way to feel more human without involving feel-ings, and Daniel had given her exactly that.

So why did her stomach twist as she watched him walk away? Why did she feel alone as she gathered her clothes and went to her room?

This was what she wanted... right?

Daniel felt like shit as he stood in the shower. How long could he keep this up? He didn't want to fuck his beautiful angel. He wanted to make love to her. He wanted to hold her and make her laugh. He wanted to tell her he loved her and never let her go.

She would stop letting him touch her if she knew how badly it hurt him, so he hid his feelings. Getting to be with her like this was better than nothing.

Even if I feel like she's turning a slow knife in my heart.

He'd known Mark had found another Immortal before the druid had even said the words, and he didn't want to think about it. Their mission put Surcy in danger. It might be the only way to show her that Caine must be overthrown, but he didn't have to like it.

And so, he'd touched her. Felt her warm body. Plunged into her tight pussy, needing to feel connected to her, if only for a moment.

The others couldn't understand—they wouldn't understand—but this is what he needed to do. It was the only way to stop him from completely losing his mind. And so, he touched her and pretended that they weren't about to step into danger again.

Turning off the water, he dried, styled his hair, and dressed. In the mirror, he saw an asshole. A man with sculpted good looks and an arrogance that hovered over him like a cloak. Most fire mages were good-looking assholes like him. Their exterior helped conceal just how dangerous they were deep inside.

His gut clenched. Going to his door, he locked it and pulled the lighter from beneath his bed.

Collapsing onto the edge of his mattress, he stared at it, flicking it open and closed. He was going nuts. Touching the fire would calm him.

But you're clean. You haven't used fire since you died. Except for when Surcy and the others begged him to call his fire to save that damn Immortal.

If I could use it then, I can use it now. Just a little.

Taking a deep breath, he rolled his thumb. Flames shot from the lighter, and he groaned. Plunging his finger into it, every hair on his body stood on end. This was power, delicious power. And he needed more of it. He wanted to coat his flesh in it and allow the warmth to curl over his body.

Surcy knocked on his door. "They're back," she said, her voice muffled.

He closed the lighter and stuffed it back under his mattress, his heart racing. He knew the door was locked, but still, he wondered, w*hat if she comes in?*

He raced to the window and opened it wide to let in fresh air, just in case. "I'll be out in a minute!"

He didn't understand Surcy's mumbled response, but he sensed her leave.

Out of danger for the moment, he perched on the window seat to regulate his breathing. His finger looked the same as before, but power hummed through it. *Fuck, that was amazing.*

But it was only a finger, and he had only used a little bit of fire. He was fine. The others didn't have to know. They wouldn't understand. No one understood how the fire called to him. Standing, he smoothed down the fabric of his well-tailored shirt and went to join them.

Out in the living room, the other three were equipping themselves with weapons. Surcy could still use her soul-blade without attracting the other angels, so she only carried a dagger on her ankle beneath her jeans. Since the demons couldn't use their special swords, they slid well-made ones into sheaths on their backs and concealed daggers wherever they could. When they were done, everyone moved closer to each other.

"Ready to go?" Mark asked.

Daniel nodded. "Do we know where and what we're facing? At all?"

Mark shook his head. "I'll send Surcy the image, and we'll teleport there. I'll know more then."

Daniel didn't like any of it, not at all. But he moved closer and took Surcy's hand, ignoring the tingle that moved through his body at her touch.

Whatever they would find there, he already knew it wouldn't be good.

Caine glared at the Fate. She was no longer just a tiny, filthy thing; instead, she was a *bloody*, filthy thing. Every day since she'd helped Sharen's demon-scum escape, he'd dragged her out into his throne room and watched as his guard beat her senseless.

Not only did she help a traitor, she allowed one of the Immortals to escape my reach. And both crimes deserved punishment... a lifetime of punishment.

Yet still, when the Fate looked at him, her bright green eyes were filled with defiance.

Will nothing break her?

She spit blood onto his polished floor and lifted her head. Her back was in shreds from his guard's whip. Her clothes had long ago fallen to pieces around her, and yet, when she opened her mouth, he knew only insolence would spout from her lips.

"Did you get off yet, Caine?"

He didn't need to send his dark magic swirling. His guard automatically whipped her again, over and over again until he heard a sob explode from her throat.

"Enough," Caine called, punctuating the command with a swipe of his hand.

She's not useful to me unconscious.

His guard stopped and stepped back, whip still in hand.

"Today is not just about your punishment," Caine said.

She didn't lift her head. "Yeah, it's about you masturbating in that fucking black shadow of yours."

His teeth ground together. "Today you will tell me how to take The God Finder from Surcy's demon."

He watched the rapid rise and fall of her blood soaked chest. "I have a feeling today I'll be bleeding in my cell, like every day."

Why must we play these games? You cannot lie, and I will get the truth from you.

He glanced up at the pale blue wisps that had gathered on the ceiling of his throne room. With the slightest gesture of his hand, the souls lowered. He neither brought them to the bright swirling hole that represented the angel-realm, nor the dark hole that represented the demon-realm. Instead, he moved them to hang above the Soul Destroyer.

Before he took the throne from the Immortal Ten, it was rarely used. A soul had to be completely unredeemable and far too dangerous to be allowed an afterlife, to be thrown into the Soul Destroyer. The place was reserved for the absolute worst beings.

He'd heard the Immortals whisper that overuse of it could throw off the balance of the realms, so he'd withheld himself. And yet, lately he had more and more difficulty not using it. When he saw a soul that was strong, confident, and capable... but would never bend to his will, he imagined what they would be like as a demon. *Just another soldier in the war against me.*

It was easier to flick them into the Soul Destroyer. When

the world didn't crumble around him, he began to accept something: the Immortal Ten may have lied about the consequences of using it too much.

And if they did, there's nothing to hold me back now.

So, when he brought the soul of a man to hoover above The Soul Destroyer, he watched the Fate's gaze move to it. The soul flowed with goodness, with strength. This man was capable of amazing things. He would never obey Caine.

He smiled. "Tell me how to get the God Finder from the druid."

The Fate struggled to climb to her feet. Her legs and arms visibly shook. She slipped in her blood, falling several times, but at last stood. "I won't keep helping you."

His smile widened. "You don't have a choice."

Turning to the soul, he made a decision there and then. He would destroy it. What did it matter? And then he'd destroy another and another, however many it took to get the Fate to obey him.

No more threats, Fate. You'll learn I'm a man without limits.

Moving his hand, he watched in satisfaction as the soul lowered closer and closer. The man began to scream as the blackness licked at him, tearing tiny pieces from him that would never exist again.

Caine closed his eyes, listening to the sound grow louder and more desperate.

"Stop it," he heard the Fate shout.

"Tell me what I wish to know," he whispered.

"And you'll save him?"

"Perhaps not him. But the next one... maybe."

Caine lowered the man even more and his blood-curdling screams were like music to his ears.

His guard shouted.

Frowning, Caine opened his eyes to see the Fate was

racing across the room. Caine opened his mouth to give an order, to do anything, but it was too late.

She slammed into the soul, shoving it free of the Soul Destroyer. To his shock, she fell into the gaping black hole. She disappeared without a sound, leaving nothing behind.

"No!" he rose from his throne and scrambled as close to the dangerous hole as he dared.

The Fate was gone.

Had a living being ever been destroyed?

His pulse raced. Now, he would no longer know the future. He wouldn't know where the angel and her demons would go next and he wouldn't know how to steal the God Finder.

And what will happen in this world without one of the Fates? The thought made his head feel light.

Something within him whispered that there would be consequences.

Balling his hands into fists, he strode back to his throne. *No!* The Fate was not essential to his plan. She was nothing more than a tool. Sometimes tools broke and had to be thrown away. Her destruction meant nothing to him. And he might not know how to take the God Finder, but—

His smile returned. The easiest answer was that he could simply torture the druid. Everyone had a breaking point. And he would make it his goal to discover the traitor's.

I haven't lost all my precious tools... there is always Surcy. He'd look forward to another late night visit of forcing himself into her mind and pulling out her secrets.

He hummed to himself as he continued judging the souls.

5

Mark's knees shook as he gripped the ancient relic that hung from around his neck and sent the image he'd seen into Surcy's mind. She stiffened for an instant as the world swept away around them. For a few precious seconds he couldn't breathe, and then they were standing in the desert, just outside of a massive city.

"Where are we?" Surcy asked, frowning.

He knew instantly, even though he wasn't sure how. "Outside of Phoenix."

"It looks like hell," Daniel grumbled.

And feels like it.

He didn't say a word, but he agreed. Already the sun was harsh overhead, and the sand stretching out until it reached the city looked miserable.

"We had better start walking," Tristan said, his tone neutral.

He's right. Even though I hate not knowing quite what trouble we'll find.

They followed Mark's lead, but instead of walking to

the city, he turned and started toward the desert. He felt the indecision of the others, but they followed slowly behind.

Because they know I'm never wrong about where to find the Immortals.

The God Finder was a gift and a curse. It helped him to know where to go, like a man moving through a dream, but it also had consequences. *Everything does.*

He didn't tell the others. They knew he was tired, but he couldn't let them know that each time he used it the artifact took some of his life force. It frightened him, but not as much as the possibility that it could kill him before he saved all the Immortals.

Then, Surcy will never be safe. Nor will Tristan, Daniel, and the other demons.

So, he pushed back the exhaustion and fear he felt each time he used The God Finder and continued forward. Because his life meant nothing when it came to the well-being of the people he loved. *And because this is what I was always destined to do.*

The desert looked harsh and unforgiving. He skirted around small mountains of rock and strange cacti. Lizards scurried past as they walked, and every few minutes he heard what sounded suspiciously like a rattlesnake. He knew this path would lead him to *her.*

They walked for hours under the harsh sun before they reached the base of a small mountain. Not far from it, they could see a paved road and a little dirt road that broke off and headed toward the mountain.

"What are these creepy things?" Daniel asked, drawing Mark's attention.

The demon pointed at little figures carved from stone that encircled the mountain, every ten feet or so. They were covered in layers of dirt and grim, yet stood straight and solid, as if cemented in place.

Tristan touched the feathers and beads that were part of the little figures. "They are art made from these lands."

"And they contain magic," Surcy added.

Daniel glanced up at her. "What kind of magic?"

"A shield. When we step through it, we'll sense the barrier created by the magic. They keep angels and other beings from teleporting in... and probably keep this place hidden from a lot of paranormal creatures."

"So the person who lives here knows magic?" Mark asked, frowning.

"Someone who lived here did," she explained. "But these are at least a couple hundred years old. I'm not sure if they put them here, or someone else."

Weird.

They started forward and instantly felt the tingle that told them a shield was indeed in place. It wasn't as powerful as the one the druids had erected around the sanctuary for the Immortals, but it would do the trick. Moving up the hill, they passed more cacti and red stone. Eventually they reached a dirt path that curved around the side of mountain, big enough to allow a car to travel up and down.

At the top, an adobe building stood silent near a beat-up car in the driveway. Neither the car nor the house looked as if they'd been used in a long time. And wide windows tinted against the bright sun appeared to watch them like eyes, but Mark sensed no movement.

Since they'd rescued two Immortals, Mark fully expected to find angels guarding every inch of this one's house.

So why weren't they?

"Uh, is this it?" Surcy asked.

Mark turned, and it took him a second to form the response. The sunlight was at her back, and it bathed her dark hair in a golden light. Even without her wings, Surcy was an angel, a being more beautiful than any woman he could imagine. And... he missed her.

She'd spent a year away from them, taken by Caine. And now that she was back, he thought that his heart would finally heal from her disappearance and he would feel full again. Instead, seeing her when she didn't remember him hurt him in an entirely new way. He tried to pretend he didn't think of her... every second of the day, but he did. Only his mission kept him sane.

"Mark?" she asked, his name holding a concerned note.

He cleared his throat. "This is her home."

"And she's a shifter?" Daniel asked frowning.

Mark nodded.

"What... like a lizard shifter? Or does she turn into rocks and dirt?"

Mark shrugged. "I'm not sure. I have all these pictures in my mind, but they don't fit here. I don't get it."

"So what should we do?" Surcy asked.

"I guess," he turned back to the house. "We knock. And keep an eye out for angels."

"Good plan," Daniel said, his sarcasm lacing each word.

Mark ignored him and started for the front door. He didn't know what he'd find inside, probably danger, but this was his best plan. Taking a deep breath, he knocked.

He heard movement inside and sensed someone on the other side of the door. For a long minute no one answered, and then he heard the sound of a chain being pulled. The door opened inch by inch, and the barrel of a shotgun appeared. He held his breath as it swung all the way open, and then, there was the woman from his visions.

Sort of. It's her... but it's not.

She was older, with long white hair, and tired eyes. She wore a nightgown and robe, both with seashells on them. And even though there was something sickly about the tone of her skin, her hands on the gun were sure.

"What can I do for you?" she asked, her eyes flashing with a challenge.

Mark held her gaze. "We're here to see you."

"Why?" she asked, her eyes running over all of them.

Damn it. Mark hadn't thought this far ahead. And he really should have.

Daniel shifted closer. "We're interested in purchasing your land." He purred the words, a big charming smile on his face.

Mark's heart raced as he looked between her gun, which was now pointed directly at Daniel's chest, and Daniel's grinning face. The fire mage was so damned cocky. Did he really think he could convince her with just a little demon charm?

It helps, but it isn't fool-proof. He knows that!

The fire mage's grin widened. "And we aren't poor chumps. We're talking about a good offer here. One that will set you up for the rest of your life."

Her gun lowered. "I'd be interested in hearing what you have to say, but this gun is staying right by my side."

"I wouldn't expect anything less, ma'am," he said.

For the first time, she smiled, then gestured for them to come in. "Sorry, the place is a mess. I've been sick for a while."

They entered the room and were surprised by the strong scent of herbs. Everything was fairly neat. On one side of the room, there sat a small seating area, with couches with little starfish on them. Bottles with ships and seashells on nearly every surface and a lamp made out of a blowfish continued the nautical theme. Around a slight corner, a kitchen table held different pill bottles and bags of herbs.

"Take a seat," she said, gesturing toward the couch.

She sat on a big chair, her knitting in a bag next to it, and rested her gun against her leg. Her hand went to a chain around her neck, and as she fiddled with it, he spotted another seashell on the end of it, this one pure white and simple. His feet froze and he stared at it until the others pushed him forward.

They awkwardly shuffled in and squeezed onto the couch, while Tristan remained standing beside them.

"Thanks for hearing us out," Daniel said, always the smooth talker. "Can you tell us a little more about your land and the history here?"

She laughed. "Well, you're the straight shooter, aren't you? Not even a 'how are you?' or 'what's your name?'"

He smiled. "Sorry, where are my manners? These are my business associates and dear friends, Tristan, Mark, and Surcy. My name is Daniel."

"I'm Mertal," she said. "Nice to meet you."

"What a lovely name," he complimented, settling back against the couch.

"Thank you. Now, you asked about these lands. Well, they've been in my family for generations. And to be honest, they've been nothing but a curse."

"A curse?" Mark asked, his instincts springing to life.

She gave a sad smile. "Every one of us has been born here. And every one of us dies here. Every time we get a chance to leave, something happens and we don't."

"That doesn't sound too bad." Mark stared at her in confusion.

Was this really the Immortal? She didn't look the way he

imagined, and yet, there was something about her that he couldn't quite put his finger on.

"It *is* bad when you want to see other things," she said, a sigh slipping past her lips. "Like the ocean. Have you ever been? I imagine the sand between my toes and the sound of the waves. I even hear them in my sleep."

Mark winced, and more images flashed through his mind. The ocean. There was something about the ocean. But what? Something wasn't adding up. Something wasn't making sense.

"You're not too far from it, just a few hours," Daniel said. "Why not just go?"

Her wistful expression faded. "Like I said, something always happens. But now, here you all come wanting to buy my lands, and I got to say, I think it might be just what I need to finally escape this place."

Mark spoke without thinking. "You believe in curses. Do you also believe there are things in this world most people wouldn't believe?"

Her gaze swung back to him, and he saw her fingers near her gun twitch. "What kinds of things?"

"Like shifters." He said the words, then stared, waiting for her response.

She threw back her head and laughed. "Like shiny vampires and werewolves and shit? You got to be kidding me, boy. I'm not some damn teenage girl."

Daniel joined in on the laughter. "Sorry, my pal here is a joker."

After a minute, she rubbed at her eyes. "Thanks, son. It's been a while since I laughed like that."

"You mentioned being sick," Surcy asked, her voice soft.

The woman's gaze moved to Surcy, and she smiled. "Yeah. The doctors can't find anything wrong with me. But

I'm always tired. My body aches. And sometimes I see things that just ain't right. They keep telling me I'm depressed. I'm not depressed. I'm sick."

"What kinds of things do you see?" Mark pressed.

She spoke after a quiet minute. "Just things that aren't right."

Mark felt that prickling again. It moved down his spine.

"Now, you mentioned an offer?"

Mark stood and moved to her window, staring out at the desert. Daniel's useless chatter drifted away. He touched The God Finder, and the world began to swim around him. The desert faded away, and he was at an ocean. A beautiful mermaid leapt from the waves and flashed him a smile. He stared at her for a long moment, and then realized why her eyes looked so familiar. *Mertal?* The old woman and the mermaid blurred together, and it hit him, they were one and the same.

Mertal was the mermaid. She was a goddess. The Goddess of the Sea.

His breathing grew more rapid. Caine didn't need to torture her with angels. Or imprison her like the vampire. He just needed to keep her away from the water. As a mermaid, she would never be free until she was in the water. She would grow old and die without ever knowing why she didn't feel right. Why her skin felt too tight.

The blurring magic of The God Finder faded away. And he gripped the edge of the windowsill to keep from falling. It was hard to breathe. Hard to pull air in and out.

At the edge of his vision, he saw shapes in the sky. *The angels are coming! How did they know we were here?*

"Guys!" he said, turning, he realized he'd stopped the conversation. Swallowing, he tried to keep his voice normal. "Lots of big birds out today."

Surcy frowned. Tristan just stared, and Daniel gave him a look like he was nuts.

"You don't see a lot of birds out here," Mertal commented, giving him a strange look.

Which is when he finally saw it hit the others.

Surcy rose. "We should go."

"But you just started talking about this offer of yours," Mertal said, wiping her palms on her gown.

Daniel stood and held out a hand to the older woman. "What she means is that we'd love a tour of your lands?"

His demon-magic swelled in the air. Perhaps it was because Mark had just used The God Finder, and every one of Mark's sense seemed heightened, but he could feel the coaxing magic sliding over her body, moving inside of her like a smoke with a purpose.

The magic was instinctual, like an angel flying. The angels couldn't detect when they used it, but they tried not to use it too often. It had the risk of someone realizing that they were doing something they wouldn't normally do and getting suspicious.

"I guess that makes sense," the woman said slowly, then grabbed her gun with one hand and took Daniel's hand with the other. "But there really isn't much to see."

She and Daniel led the way.

Surcy dropped back beside him. "I can't teleport out of here either."

He nodded. "There's something strange about this place. But, we can't worry about that now. We need to get her to the ocean."

"The ocean?" Surcy frowned. "Which one?"

"Any one." He picked up his pace, his gut tightening as they opened the front door.

The angels were getting closer. It'd be a race to see who reached the border of the shield first.

"This is my garden," Mertal laughed. "Well, an Arizona garden anyway."

She held Daniel's elbow, and he tugged her toward the path leading down the mountain. "Why don't you show us down there first?"

A cough exploded from her lips. "Alright. But slowly. The dust makes my cough worse."

Mark's tension grew like a ball in his chest. They didn't have time to hobble down the hill. He counted... eight angels coming right at them. All of them were equipped with weapons, but he wasn't sure it would be enough. To fight, yes? To get the woman and Surcy out safely, he doubted it.

"Let's speed up," Mark said, trying to swallow down his panic. "We have another... eh... appointment soon."

The older woman made a noise of disapproval. "Young people are always in such rushes."

Daniel continued to speak to her in a low voice, but their pace picked up. They wove around the hill and finally reached the ground at the same time as the angels. The eight massive men struck the ground, folded their wings and hid them with a glamour, then revealed themselves to the woman.

She cried out. "Where the hell did you come from?"

One of the angels was familiar. *Frink. Of course's it's fucking Frink. How many times do we have to kill this asshole?*

"Well," the angel began, his long, dark hair falling forward to hide part of his cruel face, "funny seeing all of you here."

Mark moved to stand in front of Surcy and grabbed the dagger from his side.

"Get out of our way," Tristan said, pulling his sword from his back. "Or do you wish to die again?"

Frink smiled. "No need to be rude. Especially when we've been kind enough to come here with a warning. This old woman just happens to have a very special curse. If she steps foot off her lands, she'll die."

"That can't be possible," Mark said. *Could it?* The woman had to have left her lands at some point in her life.

The older woman raised her gun and pointed it at Frink. "I don't know what you're talking about, but you better head out of here."

"You've left your home, right?" Surcy asked, touching Mark's arm.

Mertal didn't look back at her. "I have... just not lately."

"Because every time she gets sicker and older," Frink said with a smile. "And one more trip out will cost her her life... or at least weaken her enough for us to take what we want."

What if he's right?

"Get out of our way."

Suddenly, Mertal spun and pointed her gun at them. "I don't know what's going on here, but I'm going to go back to my house, and none of you are going to stop me."

I have to believe that I wasn't sent here for nothing. If I'm right, we just need to get her to the water.

"You have to come with us," Mark insisted.

She pointed her gun at Mark, eyes narrowing.

Daniel swore and stepped in front of Mark, reaching for her weapon.

The sound of her gun going off echoed around them. Mark's gaze moved to Daniel, and his jaw dropped. She'd shot him, right through the chest.

"I—I," she stuttered.

Surcy raced to Daniel's side and caught him as he fell. Blood drenched his chest and stomach. More blood splattered their entire group.

That won't kill Daniel, but not having his help against the angels might kill all of us.

"He reached for me," the old woman added, lamely.

Tristan grabbed her gun and tossed it onto the desert floor. "If you wish to live, you will leave with us. If you remain, these men will kill you."

Mertal paled. "But—"

Daniel fully expected the angels to attack in that moment. But they didn't. They remained on the other side of the barrier, glaring.

"What are they waiting for?" he whispered to Surcy.

She looked up from where she held Daniel. "I don't think they can cross the barrier."

That makes no sense. Surcy could.

The old woman spoke, voice shaking. "My papa always said that it kept out anyone who wished to do us harm. Maybe he wasn't so crazy."

Mark looked at the little stone statues encircling her property. Perhaps their magic was stronger than he imagined.

Tristan moved to stand closer to him. "What do we do now?"

"We need to get her to the ocean. But Surcy can't teleport us out until we get to the other side."

"So, you and I shall fight them, and she will get Daniel and the woman to safety."

It was the perfect plan. The angels wanted the Immortal and Surcy. If they could get them to safety, Mark and Tristan could handle the rest.

Mark nodded. "I guess it's our only choice."

Tristan slid to Surcy's side, whispering to her in a low tone.

Frink followed the exchange with narrowed eyes. "You're making a mistake. You have no idea how bad of one."

"And of course we trust the word of one of Caine's thugs," Mark said, anger rising within him.

Frink smiled, a smile that sent shivers running down his spine. "Don't say I didn't warn you."

"Help me with him," Surcy asked the old woman.

Mertel complied, her gaze wide.

They got him standing, braced on their shoulders. His face was pale. His expression grim. Demons might heal from almost anything, but it didn't mean it didn't hurt like hell.

Surcy looked at them and nodded.

Tristan shifted into a fighting stance, and Mark did the same. Then, Tristan transformed. His skin became the color of wet stone, and his stone wings formed on his back. Power flowed from him. Mark's chest squeezed. He longed for his druid's staff, but such a thing was nothing more than a dream.

This sword will have to do.

They stared at the angels. Their enemies called their glowing soul-blades into their hands and glared. Tension sung between them.

He and Tristan moved slowly, crossing the barrier a short distance from the angels.

Instantly, they attacked. Tristan stood his ground, striking sword after sword as if he were a titan of old. Mark fought differently, moving, and weaving through them with the grace of a druid. The angels were fast, and strong, but even though two demons could have never survived against them, they were more than just demons. And they wouldn't go down easily.

Mark was surprised when Surcy teleported away behind them with the old woman and Daniel. None of the angels rushed after them. In fact, none of them seemed to care.

An angel sliced his arm. He swore and rolled, prepared for the next attack. Two angels lifted off the ground. His gaze moved from them to the one who rushed him.

Tristan roared and severed the head from one of the angels. Then, the gargoyle turned to face the next opponent, his expression enraged.

Mark parried one sword and sent his blade through the chest of another angel. As he began to pull his weapon back, a sword went through his chest from behind. His blade slipped from his fingers, and blood spurted from his lips.

An angel's arm came around his throat.

"We got you," Frink whispered into his ear.

The world swirled as he was teleported away.

6

Surcy pulled Daniel and the woman with her to the ocean, erasing her teleporting trail, so that the angels couldn't follow them. When she felt sand beneath her feet, she was breathing hard from the exertion. Opening her eyes, she stared at a sea of brilliant blue waters.

Her gaze moved to look all around them. White sands stretched out in the other directions. Empty of any kind of intelligent life.

Thank goodness, we're safe!

Daniel sank from her shoulders, falling onto the ground. She looked down at him, her fingers itching to comfort him, but he forced a grim smile.

"Don't worry, I'm fine."

Of course that's what he'd say while bleeding everywhere.

Deep down she knew he'd heal, but he didn't have to act like it was nothing more than a scratch. She longed to ease his pain, if only by a little bit.

But I doubt he'd let me.

And then, she heard someone gasping. Turning to the

old woman, she saw that Mertal was grabbing her chest, dragging in deep breaths, her eyes wide in panic.

Please, no...

"Are you alright?" Surcy asked, hesitantly touching the woman's shoulder. Hoping she was just terrified after shooting a man, seeing a fight, and being teleported by an angel.

A terrified human I can handle. A curse? Not so much.

But this was not just terror. Mertal continued to gasp and grab her chest, her gaze growing more distant with each passing second.

Something was wrong, and Surcy had no idea how to fix it.

"What do we do?" she asked, but when she turned to Daniel, he'd passed out in the sand.

Panic clenched her heart. "Mark said you'd be fine, if we just took you here, so why aren't you?"

Surcy didn't understand, and her head felt light. The sun's rays seemed to grow more intense overhead as she struggled to decide what to do.

The old woman collapsed, her knees sinking into the wet sands along the shore. Her face growing paler. Her eyes closing.

"What do I do?" she asked again, looking around. But for the first time, she found herself with no one to guide her. *Should – should I teleport us back?*

No, they'd be right back in the angel's hands, but she couldn't just let Mertal die either.

Taking Mertal's hand, she knelt down. "I don't know what to do. You're some kind of goddess. Taking you here should have saved your life, but I don't know what else to do."

Mertal coughed and struggled to speak. "At... least... I got to see... the ocean."

Surcy looked from her to the water. Some instinct she didn't understand kicked in, and she swept the woman into her arms. Carrying her out into the water, she continued moving until the waves reached her chest.

The older woman smiled. Her breathing slowed. "I'm in the water. It feels... as good as I always imagined. After all of my dreams about the water, none of them compared to this."

She smiled, grateful the water seemed to be helping the human.

And then, Mertal grabbed the seashell around her neck. "Let me go!"

Surcy frowned. "But—"

"Let me go!" And now, her voice held power.

Surcy obeyed, releasing the woman. Mertal sank beneath the water. Waves crashed over them, and Surcy lost sight of her under the water. When the foam cleared, the older woman was gone.

Her heart sank. "Mertal? Mertal!"

Looking around herself in a panic, she dove beneath the waves. Over and over again she searched, but there was no one to be found. Time stretched out, and still, there was no sign of her.

Staring in fear at the beach, she saw that the waves had reached Daniel. Stomach turning, she slogged through the water and onto the beach. Dragging Daniel further from the water, she stroked his hair while he lay in her lap. Then, pulled back his shirt to see his wound. Already the skin was pulling together, and the bleeding had stopped.

You'll be back to yourself in no time.

And yet, she had lost the goddess they'd worked so hard

to save. She felt sick, her stomach twisting and turning like a wild animal.

I've got to go back and get Mark and Tristan. She just hoped she could grab both of them and safely escape.

Something splashed in the water. Stiffening, she sat up and looked out at the waves. There was nothing... and yet, she'd seen something.

Another splash, and this time she was sure she'd seen a tail.

Gently setting Daniel's head in the sand, she stood and walked back to the edge of the water. A minute later, a woman rose above the waves. Her hair was the color of the sun's rays, and her eyes were the shade of a clear ocean. Her shoulders were bare, and her skin pale. She hummed with power.

An immortal creature.

Surcy moved closer, as if compelled by a force more powerful than herself. When she nearly reached the woman, she saw the seashell necklace hanging around her throat.

"Mertal?" she whispered.

The woman smiled. "Mertal... yes, that was my human name. The name I held when I was imprisoned." She swam closer until she was only a foot from Surcy. "But that's not who I am. I'm the Goddess of the Ocean, Queen of the Merpeople."

Surcy's eyes widened. "A mermaid?"

She flicked her tail, and her blue and green scales sparkled in the morning light. "Does an angel truly not believe in mermaids?"

Surcy felt her cheeks heat. "I'm sorry, my queen."

The mermaid inclined her head in the most regal way

imaginable. "Thank you. Thank you for returning me to the waters and bringing back my memories."

She looks so happy. Too bad she can't stay here.

Surcy stiffened at the thought and took a deep breath before speaking. "Caine and his followers will come for you again. There's a sanctuary we need to take you too."

The queen reached out and touched her cheek, her hand ice cold against Surcy's skin. "I will never leave the waters until I return to my throne in Zudessa. But take heart, we will be prepared for Caine this time."

Surcy nodded, her words caught in her throat.

"You have no idea what it was like to slowly die in a mortal shell, far from my waters. It wasn't just my body that faded with each day, so did my connection to the ocean. Caine sought to break it from me and take my powers. Over many lifetimes he tried various ways to take my powers, but he didn't know how. This time, he understood. That should frighten you and your demons. Somehow, Caine has figured out the secret to stealing our gifts. Each of us is different, but this is the lifetime I think he may be successful."

Surcy swallowed the lump in the back of her throat. "Thanks for the warning."

The mermaid dropped her hand and smiled. "You're lucky you're no longer under his control. Even though I can feel your heart aches at the loss of your wings."

Surcy felt her heart give a painful squeeze.

"Believe me," the mermaid said, sinking into the waters. "Nothing is worth the price of your freedom."

She swam away, her beautiful tail flicking the water as she dove and played within it. Surcy held her breath, transfixed by the power of the Immortal. She was so lovely, and her happiness at being back where she belonged seemed to radiate from within her.

She's happy.

Surcy envied her. She still had no idea where she belonged.

Reality came sweeping back to her, and she turned back to the shore. Walking out of the water, she checked on Daniel one more time, then took a deep breath. She needed to snag her demons and teleport back as quickly as she could. And this trip had already taken far longer than she'd planned.

Hold on, boys, I'm coming.

The world shimmered around her as she returned to the desert. Her soul-blade leapt into her hand as she appeared where she'd left her angels and demons... only, the angels were gone. And so was Mark. Only Tristan remained, his expression grim.

"What—?"

"They took Mark," Tristan said, his tone one of complete disbelief.

"Why?"

He shook his head. "I don't know, but I think they were after him all along."

After Mark? That doesn't make sense. What could they possibly want from him?

She closed her eyes and felt for the angel's trail. The one that would tell her where they had teleported to, but they'd erased it, as expected.

Opening her eyes, she tried to hide her terror. "I can't sense where they went, so what do we do now?"

"Bring me to Daniel and the goddess."

She reached out and took his hand.

His large hand felt warm and comforting as he squeezed hers. "Everything will be okay. Mark is tougher than he appears."

She hoped so, because she was beginning to realize something horrible. Caine and his angels didn't seem to know how to be merciful. That wasn't good, not when they'd taken the demon she was growing to care for.

Please be okay, Mark. Please. We're coming as fast as we can!

7

Mark landed hard on the ground, coughing blood, and trying to calm his swimming head. One minute he'd been in the desert fighting, and now... what had happened?

We teleported.

Damn it! That can't be good!

He sensed the angels looming over him and fought his panic. They'd taken him? But why?

How can I help the others if I'm not with them?

Gritting his teeth, he willed himself to be strong, but he felt awful. Not at all prepared to fight for his life against impossible odds. Wearily his gaze moved over the strange place they'd teleported into.

Am I in a temple?

He squinted against the bright light that filtered from high above him and peered into the darkness of the room. Moss crept along the ground and walls of the grey brick that made up the building, and the air was tinged with salt. But otherwise, he had no clues as to where he was. The large room was empty, and there were no sounds of civilization that he could hear.

So I'm near the ocean. Well, that doesn't bode well for an escape attempt.

He shifted slightly and clenched his teeth together to stop himself from crying out. Warmth oozed from the wound on his chest and his arm. As a demon, he could heal from such injuries, but he'd need to rest.

Not fight five angels.

Looking up at them, he watched as Frink moved closer and knelt down in front of him. With his injuries he didn't even have the strength left to scoot away from Frink. He lay there, helpless.

Frink looked Mark up and down and then spat on the dirty stone floor beside him. "I expected more from a druid."

Mark's hand shook as he wiped the blood from his mouth. "Sorry to disappoint."

Frink's smile chilled Mark to his core. "Where's the necklace?"

Fuck. "Necklace?"

"The God Finder."

Mark's heart slammed against his rib cage and it took everything he had not to look down at the magical necklace he wore. The angels couldn't see it, nor could Caine. How did they learn about it? And how did they know he had it?

Even while the questions swirled through his head, he knew it didn't matter. All that mattered was making sure it didn't end up in their hands. If they got it, he couldn't find the Immortals and couldn't save them. Everything they'd sacrificed would be for nothing.

"I don't know what you're talking about," he said, as calmly as he could manage.

Frink's smile widened. "I bet we could get it by severing your head."

A couple of the angels snickered behind him.

Mark's vision swayed. He'd lost too much blood. He needed to rest or he'd never heal.

"Like I said, I don't know what you're talking about."

Frink's soul-blade appeared in his hand. "This might surprise you, but I'm accustomed to getting what I want. By the time I'm done with you, you'll tell me whatever I want to know."

A shiver ran down his spine. "Do what you have to, but I don't have the information you're looking for."

Frink raised a brow. "Either way, I'll have some fun. Boys, let's see how much damage we can do before we kill him."

Mark closed his eyes. He'd already died once. He'd do it again if he had to in order to save the world.

Even if it was a slow, painful death.

8

Surcy and Tristan sat on the beach, watching the waves, with Daniel still passed out between them. The afternoon temperature was perfect. A slight breeze carried the scents of vegetation and salt water, and the waves crashing against the shore were almost soothing... if they weren't sitting with a gravely injured man and trying to figure out what to do about the one who had been kidnapped.

"Tristan, we can't just do nothing!" Surcy said, turning to the gargoyle in frustration.

Tristan looked at her, and for a minute his cold mask slipped. "He's my best friend and like a brother to me. We died around the same time. We were reborn together. It took us years of working together to climb up through the pits of the demon-realm. Without him, a piece of myself is gone. But, we don't know where they took him, and we don't know how to find him. We just have to trust that he can find his way back to us."

Surcy took a deep breath. "No, that's just not good enough."

He raised a brow. "Then, what do you suggest we do?"

She picked up a handful of sand and threw it. "I don't fucking know."

When she looked at him again, he was smiling.

"What?"

"You're swearing again. Like yourself before you were taken."

She felt her cheeks heat. *Probably because I've been having sex with Daniel.* "I'm just so frustrated! I feel helpless, but we're not. There has to be something we can do!"

The truth was she was also feeling guilty. She'd grown to care for Mark. He fascinated her. With his glasses and laid back attitude, he felt like a friend she could trust. But when she saw him with a towel wrapped around his waist, and water dripping down his chest. She felt... aroused as hell. He was a handsome, kind man. Even though she didn't remember loving him, she could imagine that he was an easy man to love.

And I did love him before.

The idea made her feel antsy. The same way she felt when the demons looked at her as if she held their hearts in her hand, as if they were imagining a thousand moments with her that she didn't remember.

Taking off her boots and socks, she stood and walked across the sand and into the water. Her clothes had finally dried from her earlier walk into the water, but she didn't care. She just needed to escape for a minute, to clear her head.

Diving under the water, she felt every muscle in her body tense as she kicked further and further out into the sea. *I'm swimming while those bastards have Mark.* Her heart squeezed, and she clenched her teeth, trying not to scream her frustration.

She needed to save Mark, but how?

Taking a deep breath, she dove back under and swam in the clear water beneath the foam of the waves. And froze. A man stared at her. No, not a man, a merman. His hair was dark, his eyes piercing, and anger swirled around him.

The water surged from him to her, swirled around her, and dragged her through the water. Panic swelled in her chest. The need for air built and built.

He's going to drown me!

And then his face was inches from hers. Leaning close, he pressed his lips against hers, and air filled her lungs. She breathed again, and although she should have breathed in water, nothing happened. She inhaled and exhaled normally. At the bottom of the sea.

This couldn't be happening.

Turning to the merman, she stared with unspoken questions.

But then, The Goddess of the Ocean swam through the waves. "Why have you returned?" she asked, power still swelling from her.

Surcy opened her mouth, and the words came out as if spoken above the water. "The angels stole Mark. We don't know where he is, or how to get him back."

The power of the goddess grew until the very water seemed to be charged with electricity. "They're after The God Finder. Your druid friend will not last the night."

And we can't save him, unless...

Heart racing, she asked the question she feared. "Can you help us find him?"

After a moment, the goddess nodded. "You saved my life and freed me. I owe you a life debt."

The water began to swirl around them. It moved faster and faster. A tornado of water rushed at them and then it pulled back. Surcy, the Goddess of the Ocean, and the glaring merman stared at one another, lying on the ocean floor in the myths of the swirling water tornado. The goddess reached down and plucked a seashell off of the sandy bottom. She held it to her lips, and wisps of blue magic moved from her to the seashell. When she was done, she offered it to Surcy.

Surcy crawled across the ground, took the seashell, and looked at the goddess in confusion.

"It will reveal its secrets to you, but be ready to act when it does."

Tears stung her eyes for reasons she couldn't explain. "Thank you."

The goddess smiled. "Hold your breath."

"My breath?"

The tornado of water came crashing down on her. She had a moment of panic as she was tumbled through the water at an impossible speed, and then she was dumped out onto the beach.

Breathing hard, she opened her hand and stared down at the shell.

Tristan was beside her in an instant. "Where were you?" He roared. "I couldn't find you!"

She looked up at him. "The goddess gave me a gift."

"A gift?"

She held out the shell.

He frowned. "You risked your life for that?"

She climbed to her feet, legs shaking, and hurried to Daniel's side. "It'll tell us how to find Mark, but first, we need to take Daniel home."

Tristan said nothing, but he took Daniel's limp hand, and then hers. They teleported, the world shimmering around them. When they arrived at their home, Tristan carried Daniel to his bed, while Surcy stripped off her sandy, wet clothes, changed, and pulled on new boots.

By the time she returned to the living room, Tristan was already waiting.

"Ready?"

He nodded.

Lifting the shell to her ear, she closed her eyes and waited.

Nothing happened.

She shook the shell, listened again, and still, nothing happened.

"It's not working."

Tristan frowned. "Mermaid gifts are never simple."

She stared at the shell in her hand. "What can we do?"

He exhaled noisily, sounding annoyed. "I have an idea."

9

Surcy and Tristan stood at the front of the small sailing boat that he had procured. She didn't know where it came from, but she didn't care. Mark's life was at stake.

Tristan moved with certainty as he took them from the dock and sailed them out into the middle of the cove. There, he dropped anchor and went to stand at her side.

"Try listening to it now."

"I tried the whole way," she insisted, but she tried again. *Still nothing.*

"Drop it in the sea."

She whirled toward him. "If this doesn't work, we've lost our only way of finding him."

"Drop it," he said, his tone unforgiving.

She felt sick as she stretched her hand out over the water. It took her a long second to open her fingers, but with a deep breath, she turned her hand over.

The shell dropped as if in slow motion, but when it hit the water, a wave boomed out. The waves rose, and suddenly, their ship was flying over the ocean like a child's toy. She clung to the edge of the ship, but her fingers began to slip. Tristan was immediately there, pulling her against him, and holding onto the railing as if it was the easiest thing in the world.

The water struck them wildly, powerfully, and still, the gargoyle held her.

Time passed. Her face rested against his chest and she breathed in the earthy scent that belonged to the gargoyle. Her eyes closed. For a minute, with the water spinning around them and the boat soaring over the waves, she felt lost in a dream. In Tristan's arms, nothing scared her. She felt safe and protected.

And this feels so natural.

How many times had his arms held her, times that she still didn't remember? How many times had he protected her? He stayed with her, beside her, through each day, even though she couldn't open up to him.

This big, strong man needed more from her. All three of her demons did. She'd thought she couldn't give it to them when she wasn't sure about their cause, the angels, or the true nature of demons. She had thought she couldn't connect with them because she wasn't sure who she was anymore, and because she didn't remember her past.

But maybe, instead, she needed to focus on creating a new connection with them. *New memories. New moments.*

Lifting her head, she whispered his name.

He looked down at her. His dark hair was soaking wet. His skin glistened with water, and yet, his mismatched eyes latched onto hers as if there was nothing else in the world but them.

Reaching up, she touched his cheek. She wanted to kiss him, but she didn't. She just clung to him and touched his face, memorizing every line.

"What do you ask of me?" he murmured, his voice barely audible above the rushing water.

"Just... just a chance to try again."

His eyes widened, and very slowly, he nodded.

A slight smile teased his lips. "I would like that very much."

When the waves calmed, they struck land. The ship pitched, and if it weren't for Tristan's strong grip, they would have gone flying into the water. Instead, they clung to each other, panting.

The ship righted itself. The waves calmed, and the ocean grew still around them.

They moved to the other side of the ship and stared at the little island. There was nothing on it except a lonely looking building made of dark stone.

"You think that's where he is?"

Tristan nodded. "I think so." Turning, she took a deep breath. *It's okay. You can handle this.* "Will you fly us over to it?"

His gaze locked onto hers. "Are you sure? We can teleport."

"I can handle it." Lifting her hands, she wrapped them around his neck.

He transformed in an instant, his flesh turning to cold stone beneath her touch, and his stone wings sprouting from his back. When he lifted them into the air, she felt the wind on her face. Flashes of herself soaring through the air came to her, and she felt herself trembling. Memories came back, of her wings being torn from her back, of the wounds that ached for too long.

When they landed on the island, he put her down.

She stumbled away from him and threw up. Dropping to her knees, tears slid down her cheeks. She didn't understand why she was reacting like this. It wasn't like her life had been easy. It made no sense.

Tristan sat down on the sand beside her and stroked her back, avoiding her scars.

Wiping her mouth, she turned to him, feeling ashamed. "I'm sorry."

He was quiet for a long moment. "In my previous life, I was a gargoyle created to defend my town. For many, many years, I came to life only when I was needed, but the time between attacks grew longer and longer, and I remained a creature of stone for too long. When I was needed again, I didn't expect to die. I didn't believe one of my kind could be killed.

I thought whatever I faced would be easy. I'd fought vampires, werewolves, cruel humans, armies... many, many battles. When I was reborn in the demon realm, I was afraid. I have never feared the dark like that before. But it was endless. And the screaming..." He paused, shaking his head. "That's why I still don't like the dark. There are times when I forget what it was like, and then something will remind me. I find my heart beating fast, and my skin dampened with sweat."

She smiled at him. "So, you're telling me this is perfectly normal?"

The corner of his mouth twitched. "Or we are both unusual."

Sighing, she looked back at the little building. "Well, I'd better pull myself together and find Mark."

He stood and held out his hand.

She shook her head, knowing she needed a minute to clear her thoughts. Rising and going to the water, she washed her face and hands. That seemed to help. She still felt embarrassed, but a little better. Ready to kick some angel ass.

I feel the way I do after Daniel and I have sex. As if my emotions and senses aren't as muted. I feel charged with energy. Almost overloaded.

Weird...

Clenching her hands, her focus returned. And something else. A feeling she hadn't experienced much since becoming an angel... that she could remember. Rage rolled through her. These angels had stolen Mark. The goddess said he wouldn't last the night.

How dare they!

"Come on," she said, calling her soul-blade to her hand. "Surcy?"

"I'm going to teach those fucking angels a lesson."

Tristan pulled his blade from his back with a hiss. "This is a plan I like."

As they started through the palm trees and plants, a horrible scream echoed through the air. Birds launched into the sky, and the very trees seemed to shake.

But the effect on the surroundings was nothing compared to what that sound did to Surcy. She recognized Mark's voice. She'd know it anywhere, and his scream was one of horrible pain.

She started running. She didn't care if she was going straight into danger. No one hurt her demon. *No one!*

10

S urcy and Tristan ran until they pushed through the growth that hid the building from view. When they drew closer, they slowed and crept to the front.

The door in the front of the building was partially ajar. She and Tristan stood on either side of the door, made eye contact and he nodded. She pushed the door all the way open and launched inside.

Inside, she discovered one big room, dark except for light that streamed from a skylight in the center. On the floor, bathed in the sun's light, Mark lay bleeding. Surrounded by angels who towered over him.

The angels' laughter came to her, and she saw red. Angels were supposed to protect the innocent from demons. That's what she'd been told. So far, she'd seen things that made her question who was actually good and evil. Something inside her changed in that moment. She felt it, like puzzle pieces sliding into place.

She no longer had wings. She no longer obeyed Caine.

The angels were her enemies now. There was no question. And her job? Her job was to protect the men who loved her for reasons she didn't understand.

She entered the room like a ghost. Moving behind Frink, she sliced his head from his neck before he could react. The angels turned to her in shock. Another head went flying.

And then, the battle began in earnest.

Their soul-blades flared to life. One blade crashed against hers. Another clashed against Tristan's.

She kicked the angel in the chest, then knocked his blade from his grip. "So, you think hurting a defenseless man is fun?"

The angel's eyes widened, and he glanced behind him to where his blade was out of reach.

She knew he was about to teleport. Striking out, he tried to leap out of the way, but she sliced his chest. He took another step back. But she wouldn't give him the second he needed to concentrate enough to teleport. Instead, she launched an attack.

He dove, jumped, and tried to avoid her blows. She was hell-bent on causing him pain. Not killing him. Making him suffer.

When he fell to his knees, his arms bleeding, his stomach bleeding, he looked up at her with pleading eyes. "Mercy," he whispered.

"Did you show Mark mercy?"

His acceptance was there in his face.

She raised her sword, and sliced his head off. It hit the ground, and then, silence stretched around her. Strange and oddly tense

Turning, she saw that Tristan had killed his angel. He was watching her, his expression unreadable. Whether the other angels had died or teleported away, she didn't know. Nor did she care. As long as they were gone.

Sending her soul-blade away, she ran to Mark.

A sob grew in her throat. His injuries were bad... bad enough that he might not survive.

Reaching out, she touched his face. His eyes flashed open, and the pain within them was heartbreaking.

"Kill me," he whispered.

Her heart pounded in her chest. "You don't mean that."

"Please."

She tore her gaze from him to Tristan. "Touch me. I'm getting us out of here."

Tristan knelt and placed a hand on her arm, obeying. She teleported them, and forced herself to erase their path so the other angels couldn't find them. It was harder. And by the time they appeared in her room, she was breathing hard.

"Help me get him in the shower and then you take care of Daniel."

Tristan plucked Mark out of her arms like he was a child and brought him to the shower, laying him down. Looking back at her, she could see for a moment his fear and anguish. "Take care of him."

"I will," she whispered.

And then, the big man left.

Shedding her bloody clothes, she entered the shower, turning on the water. Mark hissed and thrashed, but she tried to shield him as much as she could while the water heated up. Then, carefully, she tore his clothes off and set them outside the shower.

The wounds that covered him were stomach-churning. The slices, careful and painful, covered every inch of his body.

"Fucking angels," she hissed.

"Kill me," he begged, his eyes squeezed shut, his chest rising and falling rapidly.

"No," she whispered, lying beside him on the massive floor of the shower, she watched as the blood washed from him, coloring the water.

He shook under her touch, but she stroked him slowly. She knew some angels were capable of healing. Of taking away pain, but she wasn't sure how. The only thing she could do was stay with him as his body worked to knit itself back together. She prayed he would fall asleep soon. He'd heal faster if he could.

But the druid didn't sleep. He pleaded in a soft, pained voice for her to end his life.

She held him in the water, pretending tears weren't running down her face.

When he finally passed out, she began to sob. No one should hurt like this. No one should beg for death. Certainly not her sweet Mark.

Never him.

Even when the water grew cold, she lay with him, watching his wounds in fear. They would heal. They had to heal. Only cutting his head off would kill him. Right?

She found herself unsure as she realized that not a single wound was closing. They remained open, bleeding, more than a body should be able to endure.

Swallowing, she pressed her forehead against his, begging him to be okay. With a soft touch, she rubbed her lips against his.

Should her heart really ache this much? Should she really feel this frightened?

Am I falling in love with him?

She thought of her demons. There was still so much she didn't understand about them. So many mysteries surrounding them. Yet, she felt something powerful for them, something that hurt for her to think about.

When she lightly kissed him again, she felt the strangest tingle pass between them. Mark shifted and groaned beneath her, not in pleasure exactly, but not in pain.

Curious, she kissed him again and again. The feeling only intensified.

When she looked down at his wounds, they'd stopped bleeding. Staring, she watched in silent wonder as they slowly began to knit back together.

Is it my kiss? Is it helping him? She wasn't sure if it was some magic she didn't understand, or the strength of their bond, but hours passed, and Mark's body was no longer a sea of wounds, but scars.

When Tristan came some time later, his gaze ran over them, lying together naked.

"Is Daniel okay?"

Tristan nodded. "He's still asleep, but his wound looks good."

She looked down at Mark's pale face. "Should we get him into bed?"

"That would be wise."

Turning off the water, they did their best to dry him, then she dried herself.

Laying him down in her bed, she touched his chest. "I think I'm going to sleep in here with him."

"He would like that."

It took her hours to fall asleep, but when she did, she didn't wake in the night drenched in sweat. Imagining Caine in her room, burning her mind. She awoke in the morning, a slight breeze moving the white curtains where her balcony doors stood open.

When she sat up slightly and looked at Mark, he was awake. His gaze met hers.

Tears stung the corners of her eyes. "You're okay."

He said nothing.

"I'm sorry. I know you were hurting. I know you wanted me to... you wanted me to—"

He reached up, his hands digging into the back of her hair, and pulled her down to him.

Their kiss was earth-shattering, a power that moved through her and him. His lips were strong, aggressive. And when his tongue dove into hers, she moaned.

This man knew how to kiss. He knew how to shatter her thoughts with his touch.

When his hand slid down her neck, trailing along the sensitive skin of her throat, and then caressed her breasts, she arched into his touch. Within seconds, his fingers brushed her nipples, and she gasped. He played with her tips as his kiss grew more intense.

With her head swimming, she pulled back. "You're hurt."

"Then, I guess you'll have to be gentle," he growled.

Her gaze met his. This was the demon. Not the gentle man or the druid, but the demon who wanted to claim what was his.

But what if she hurt him?

As if in answer, his hand moved from her breasts, sliding over her belly.

She tensed as he stroked her womanhood, and then one finger moved inside of her. He stroked her slowly, sending her nerves exploding in little bursts. When he moved into her opening, she spread her legs wider, whimpering.

Her eyes closed, and she arched against him. Her release was so close, building like something powerful.

And then she realized something, he was the one who had been through so much. Not her. She should make him feel like this. Not the other way around.

Opening her eyes, she pushed his hand away.

"Surcy?"

Pulling the sheet down, she revealed his massive erection. Swallowing, she stared and stared. She hadn't known what to expect from the shy man. But this was not it.

"God, how do you fit that into normal pants?"

He chuckled, a low aroused sound that was completely unexpected.

Kissing his chest, she lightly brushed her lips against all of the still-healing scars.

He groaned and buried his hand in the back of her hair.

She moved slowly down until she reached his delicious cock. Unable to help herself, she trailed her fingertips against the length, glorying in how long and thick he was. Then, sliding her tongue along the sides of him, she continued her exploration, loving the sound of his panting.

When she came to his tip, she looked up, meeting his gaze, then licked him.

"Fuck, Surcy, it's been too long. You can't just—"

In answer, she parted her lips and took him into her hot mouth.

A string of curses left his mouth, which only turned her on more.

She took him as deep as she could, then gagged around him when his tip hit the back of his throat. Reaching down, she cupped his balls, rolling them in her hand, while she hummed around him.

"Fuck, fuck, fuck!" he groaned, one of his hands slamming against the bed.

And then, she pulled back and slid him back in, over and over again.

With a roar, he grabbed the back of her head and began to fuck her mouth. His possessive control turned her on in a way she never expected. She felt like a creature made to pleasure him, and she ached to taste him as he exploded into her mouth.

But as she felt him swelling in her mouth, her nails digging into his thighs, he suddenly pulled her back, his cock slipping out of her mouth.

"Come on, come ride my cock."

She trembled as she climbed over him and positioned his tip at her entrance.

He pulled her down, taking one of her nipples into his mouth and sucking, while his hand plucked at her other nipple.

She moaned and sank his tip into her. Inch by inch she took him in, her tight body squeezing around him. When she reached his hilt, he released her breasts.

He held her gaze as he reached between them with one big hand and began to stroke her clit.

She gasped, her body shuddering around his big shaft, and then she started to ride him.

He thrust back, taking her deep and hard. He moved like a man hell-bent on claiming her as his own. She could feel it with each stroke.

And she felt like a woman who had given herself to a man. Who accepted his claim over her without question. Which was strangely satisfying.

She gripped his shoulders harder, riding her orgasm like a wave. Her entire body alive. Every nerve sensitive and pulsing with pleasure.

When he came with a ragged roar, she gloried in the feeling of his hot cum coating her insides. For a long minute they continued to fuck, until at last she collapsed on top of him.

His hands grabbed her ass and shoved her harder onto his erection.

She whimpered, her head still spinning in ecstasy.

"You're mine," he growled, his words were low and harsh.

She should've been scared, but she wasn't. When she'd seen him hurt, her heart had ached in a way it never had before. She wasn't sure if she loved him yet, but she felt connected to him. She cared about him in a deep way.

And now, they'd made love.

She smiled, closing her eyes. She wanted him to hold her forever. And with the way he clung to her, she was sure he felt the same way.

This is the first truly beautiful thing I've experienced since dying... that I can remember. I think I know why I gave up heaven and my wings for these demons.

11

Daniel woke up feeling like shit, but as much as he wanted to go back to sleep, he needed to see Surcy. He needed to know she was safe.

Tristan snored in a chair beside his bed, looking haggard.

Not wanting to wake him, he eased cautiously out of bed and padded on bare feet across the wooden floor. Outside of Surcy's bedroom door, he only hesitated a moment before turning the handle and opening it. He took two steps in, his gaze moving to the bed, and froze.

She was asleep on top of Mark. They were both naked, and her arms were wrapped around his neck.

Daniel couldn't pull in a breath. He stared and stared, unable to believe what he was seeing. This wasn't a quick fuck. This was something more.

Stumbling back out the door, he didn't stop until his back hit the wall of the hallway. Sinking to the floor, he lay there. How many times could this little angel break his heart? How was he to endure the fact that he was nothing but a hard cock to her, and Mark was a man she clearly cared for?

I can't. I can't endure this. If she can't love me, I don't have a reason to keep breathing.

Something wild came over him. He hurried back to his room, dressed in silence, wincing as his wound ached with each movement, grabbed his lighter, and headed out the door. He didn't look back.

It was night. And the streets were dark. A coldness had settled over the city.

One he liked.

He walked for hours, until he reached the edge of town, then further. He kept moving until a prickling at the back of his neck made him turn and start walking through the woods. After several minutes, he tore free of the trees and stared out at the abandoned house.

It was perfect.

He walked to it. Pushed passed the half-broken door and looked around the broken floor boards. No one had been in this place for a long time.

Closing his eyes, he grabbed his lighter from his pocket and opened it. A flick of his thumb later, a flame leapt to life. Sending it a simple command, he watched, every hair on his body rising, as the flame moved over his hand. It felt so damn good, warm and powerful. For a second he just felt it, and breathed in the scent of smoke.

And then, he opened his eyes and smiled. The flames poured over his palm and down onto the old wood. Within seconds, the smell of burnt wood hit his nostrils. The fire spread like a wild creature until the floors burned, then the torn curtains, and the ceiling.

He raised both hands, letting the flames run over him and through him. His power swelled, building with an intensity that made him groan. This is what he needed. Not Surcy's love. Not his bond with Mark and Tristan. *This!*

A small voice whispered at the back of his mind. *Fire is what killed you in your first life. Do you really want to do it again?*

He pushed the thoughts away. Last time he was young and reckless. This time, he'd be careful.

Standing in the fire, he waited until every board burned away, until there was nothing but a raging fire. He sensed the flames eagerness to spread to the woods around them. The thought made him shudder. What would it be like to burn down the entire forest?

But with reluctance, he controlled his fire. Creating such a big fire would draw the attention of dangerous beings. He had to keep this to himself, enjoy it on his own, without consequences.

When every last piece of wood was gone, he gritted his teeth and smothered the fire.

Breathing hard, he looked at his skin. It almost glowed with his power. And God did he love it!

A shiver ran down his spine. He continued walking until he found a river. There, he washed himself, trying to rid himself of the smell of smoke.

When he was done, the sun had risen. He made the slow trek home feeling energized. Even his wound no longer hurt.

He might not have Surcy. He might resent Mark. But now, now he felt that he could face it all without crumbling inside.

When he reached their apartment, everyone was seated at the table.

Surcy turned nervous eyes onto him. "Where were you? We were worried."

"And what happened to your clothes?" Mark asked.

He walked past them, swallowing down his anger. "Can't a man go for a walk without you two jumping down his throat?"

Going to his room, he closed the door, locked it, and tossed his clothes in the basket. In the shower, he scrubbed until he was sure all hints of what he had done were gone. Styling his hair and changing, he stared at himself in the mirror. No one would have a clue what he'd done.

They had their secrets. Well, now he had his.

At the table, he swallowed down his tasteless coffee and eggs and waited.

"As soon as we heal up, we need to search for the other Immortal I saw." Mark began, sounding tired and sore.

He should have rested instead of fucking Surcy.

"You're the boss," he said. "Just tell us what to do."

He could feel more than one gaze cling to him, but he didn't care. Once Mark found them the next Immortal, Daniel would show Surcy what he was capable of. And maybe she'd realize he was more than just a good lay.

That's not how you won her heart last time. He pushed the treacherous thought aside, clenching his teeth. None of that mattered, because Surcy didn't remember that.

Rising from the table, he put his dishes in the sink.

"How are you feeling?" Tristan asked, and he could sense the worry behind the stoic gargoyle's question.

He didn't meet the other man's gaze, he was just too damn observant. "A little sore, but I'll live."

Heading for his room, he decided to check with his human team. He'd hired them to monitor his stocks and investments when he didn't have time to do it himself. They were good. Damn good. But it'd been longer than usual since he'd talked to them last.

When he reached his room, he seated himself at his desk and pulled out his cellphone.

There was a knock at his door.

Fuck.

"Come in."

Surcy slipped in. It was impossible not to look at her. She was so damn beautiful. Her hair still damp from a shower. Her cheeks flushed with good health. She'd changed so much since she'd returned from Caine. Each day she looked more like her old self, but that made it even harder to remember that everything had changed between them.

"I just," she stared, hesitating. "I wanted to see how you were really doing. I didn't get to see you much after we got back."

He tried to keep the anger out of his voice. "Well, you were busy with Mark."

She stiffened. "He was worse off, and Tristan was taking care of you."

Tilting his head, he stared at her. "Whatever you have to tell yourself, babe."

Something flashed in her eyes. "Look, I'm sorry. I should have come by, but I'm here now."

How helpful. "Don't worry your pretty little head about it. I'm not like Mark. I don't need you fussing over me like I'm helpless."

"He wasn't helpless. He was just—"

He crossed his arms over his chest. "Like I said. I didn't need you here. In fact, I don't need you for much. I'm a fucking demon who can take care of his own damn self."

Now he was sure it was anger in her eyes. "Why are you being such an ass?"

"I know since you got back you've gotten used to us all

focused on you, but I think you're strong enough now that I don't have to coddle you anymore. If that makes me an ass, then I guess I'm an ass."

Her hands planted on her hips. "I never needed you to coddle me!"

He smirked. "Look, I have some work to do. Maybe Mark is fine dealing with your hysterics, but I don't have the patience for it."

"You're an asshole," she hissed, then turning, she stomped out the door.

When it shut, he sank back in his chair. Why did his entire chest ache? He rubbed at it, staring at the door. He needed to call his team. He needed to keep busy, but he just kept staring at the door, wondering what he was supposed to do.

There was no way he could let Surcy know how much she hurt him. He would keep her at arm's length for a while, until he licked his wounds a bit. He knew logically everything he'd done made perfect sense.

So why did it feel so wrong?

When I was alive, women told me I was unlovable. Surcy made me believe they were wrong. But maybe she was just crazy.

I don't even love myself.

12

Surcy dressed in jeans and a black shirt. While she was putting on her boots, she looked at her reflection in the mirror. Her clothes were getting tight. Instead of hanging off of her, they were hugging her curves. She couldn't decide if it was sexy, or just meant she needed to get some new clothes.

Daniel would probably say the latter.

Anger flared within her. She was so sick of his attitude. She didn't know what the hell crawled up his butt, but she had started avoiding him like the plague.

There was a knock at her door.

A smile touched her lips. Mark always knocked, even though he'd been sharing her bed since he'd been hurt.

"Come in!"

But when the door opened, it was Tristan. "May I speak to you a moment?"

She nodded, as a tingle moved down her spine. This man did things to her. Every time she looked at his big hands, she thought of what they felt like touching her.

When he spoke, her gaze was glued to his mouth, remembering what his kiss was like.

And she hated that she wasn't able to hide her thoughts better.

He seated himself at the little white chair in front of her vanity. Looking like an adult squeezing into a kid's chair.

She smiled. How could such a big man be so quiet? So gentle?

"I would like to discuss Daniel."

Her happiness fled, and every muscle in her body tensed. "Why?"

"He is not himself, and I feel the change has to do with something that happened between the two of you."

She raised her chin. "I didn't do a thing. The guy just has a giant stick up his ass that someone needs to help him remove."

Tristan lifted a brow. "Daniel is volatile. All fire mages are, but something triggered his mood."

"You'd have to ask him about that!"

The big man sighed. "You too have been having sex for some time."

It took her a minute to realize her mouth was hanging open before she closed it. "You knew?"

He shrugged. "It wasn't hard for an astute observer to notice."

Her heart raced. "We worried you guys would be mad."

"Mad?" he shook his head. "I would not be mad that my good friend and the woman we love were having sex. I would caution you about taking such an action with him though. As you have seen, Daniel's feelings run deeply, and he is not good at handling them."

"Us having sex didn't start this."

He didn't look convinced. "How much time have you and Daniel spent getting to know each other?"

She felt her cheeks heat. "I mean, we live together, so it isn't like we're strangers."

"Two people can live together and not know one another. Think about roommates. About loveless marriages. Connecting with someone takes time and energy."

Something about his words made her uncomfortable. "I guess we don't know each other all that well, but we do know each other."

"So he spoke to you of his difficult childhood and of his many failed relationships?"

She stiffened. "No, I guess... I didn't really think about it."

Tristan was silent for a long minute. "Fire mages are rare. From a young age they are sensitive. They cry often, anger easily, and sleep little. Most are given away. Like Daniel, who grew up in many different foster homes. But unlike most mages, he did not understand what he was until he became an adult. He had no one to guide him in his magic and no one to warn him."

"Warn him?" she repeated, clenching her hands in her lap.

"Fire fuels fire mages. It makes them stronger and more powerful, but it also makes them crazed. Like a drug addict needing their next fix. They can function normally, using their magic just when needed, but it takes a lot of time and training... which Daniel was never given. He grew to be a man who was passionate. Successful in business. He had cars, homes, and material possessions. Many 'friends' clung to him at clubs as he showered them in gifts and liquor. But he had few who truly cared for him."

Tristan stared off for a moment, as if lost in thought.

"When he describes his life, it is first with a zest for all the things he had. But in quiet moments, he describes a very lonely man, desperate for human companionship. He reached for women to make him feel whole, but none knew him well enough to see the broken child within him. When they walked away, it only made him feel more worthless. And so, he turned to his fire more and more. But a fire mage cannot endure the flames forever. And one day they killed him."

"I—I had no idea."

"When we journeyed together in the demon realm, he reached for fire every time he hurt. And we would stop him. We were there for him. His friends no matter what side of himself he showed. The day he realized we would not abandon him no matter what, he broke. Never had he imagined that people could see his flaws and still love him."

Her eyes stung. "That's awful."

"I am protective of Daniel in a way that I am not of Mark. Mark is a man who has known love. Who has known kindness. And even though he has also been hurt and known cruelty, he can process his feelings in a way Daniel cannot. When I see you with Daniel, I see a side to you that I do not like. I feel that you have not taken the time to see him for who he is, and you crush him with a reckless cruelty you do not understand."

"That's not true!" she argued.

Tristan held up a hand. "Sensitive people lead difficult lives. They either find people who treasure how precious that is, or they find a way to hide who they are from the world in fear. He has many, many defenses to protect how vulnerable he is. And you, a woman he loves, can smash those defenses with a wave of your hand."

"I never try to hurt him," she said, but the fight was out of her voice.

"But you do," he stared. "And sometimes intention means less than action. Your actions are cruel. Even if you don't remember our lives together, we do. Use your empathy."

"I tried to talk to him..."

He cocked his head. "And that is enough for you? You feel that you have done enough to be kind to someone who loves you?"

"Damn," she muttered. "You really know how to make a person feel like crap."

He frowned. "I am being kind to you. If you were another woman, I would have taken greater action for hurting my friend so badly."

"Like beating her up?" She asked with a grin.

"Beating?" His jaw dropped. "I do *not* beat women!"

She couldn't stop the laugh that exploded from her lips. "It was a joke."

He rose. "Your humor is... awful."

That made her laugh harder. "I wasn't saying you beat women! Just joking about what you do to protect Daniel!"

He crossed the room and planted his hands on both sides of the bed beside her. She was forced to lean back with his face inches from her own. "The only woman I have hit was you, when you begged me to spank you. Hard."

Her cheeks grew hot. "I have not!"

His mouth quirked. "You have. And you will again."

She leaned in, desperate for his kiss.

He stood, his cock level with her mouth. "Think about that, sweet Surcy."

When he turned and left, it took her a long minute to remember to breathe. *Damn sexy gargoyles!*

And then, she thought of their conversation. Daniel seemed so... angry and tough. Was it really possible that she was hurting him? She'd started to imagine that he had never really loved her, or that maybe he couldn't love who she was now. But if she accepted what Tristan said... and Daniel loved her but was just too broken to show her that he did, well, she was a complete ass.

She rose and froze. What would she say to him?

Something in her chest ached to find him. Her thoughts kept flashing to the man Tristan described. Someone who had never really known real love other than with her. If she could go to here and now and declare her feelings for him, she would. *But do I know how I feel?*

Instead of running to his room, she went to her balcony and stared out at Mark's carefully tended garden, and beyond the treetops to the city that surrounded them. "Damn it, if only I could remember!"

Frustration blossomed within her. It wasn't fair! If she could just remember, then she could honestly tell him she loved him. But as of now? She felt something for him... but it wasn't love yet, and she couldn't lie to him. Going to him now, what could she offer him? Pity.

Daniel wouldn't want that.

She hated how helpless that made her feel.

So, she remained rooted in place, her hands clenched around the railing. Her mind far away—with a demon she wasn't sure she'd ever understand.

No matter how much she wanted to.

13

The sound of someone knocking at Surcy's door filtered out to the balcony. Exhaling slowly, she willed herself to be ready for whatever she might face next, then turned and walked back into her room. "Come in."

Mark entered, and she swore he looked worse than before. *Is he losing weight?*

"Did you use it again?" She hadn't intended it, but the words came out harshly, almost as bad as an accusation.

He winced. "Yes."

"And you've found another Immortal?"

He nodded.

"Maybe… maybe this time just Daniel and Tristan and I should go," she offered, knowing it would change nothing.

He drew himself up taller. "I'm fine."

"No, you're—"

"None of you could find him without me, so this is how it is. There's no use in discussing it."

She wanted to argue, but she bit her lip.

"Can you join us at the table?" He held out his hand.

She smiled at the simple gesture and went to him, taking the hand he offered. Instantly, a tingle ran between them, and she moved closer, planting a kiss softly on his lips.

He looked down at her, his blue eyes filled with happiness. "I can't believe you're real."

She touched the stubble on his chin. "Of course I am."

"It's just... sometimes when I look at you, all I can think about was the first time we met, how the sun bathed you in light. How we were all worried you'd find out what we were and send us back to the demon-realm."

Her smile faded. "I wish I remembered."

"I do too." His gaze ran over her. "It's strange to have a whole lifetime of moments with you, and for you to remember none of it. I keep trying to push them away, but they're still there."

"I wonder which of us this is stranger for."

He tilted his head. "It's painful to remember, but I'd never want to forget."

She kissed him again, overwhelmed with sadness. "Shall we join the others?"

He nodded and tugged her gently out of the room, his hand still holding hers.

At the table, Daniel and Tristan were eating massive sandwiches, with chips piled high on their plates. When Daniel looked up, his gaze moved to their held hands. He put his sandwich down and stared at his plate.

Suddenly, she felt uncomfortable. She was glad when Mark released her hand and sat down at the table.

"I've found another Immortal. And there's possibly more of them. But there's a catch."

"Isn't there always?" Daniel grumbled.

Mark ignored him. "The next Immortal... I think he may be a dragon."

"Dragon?" Tristan frowned. "That should be no great problem. Dragons walk among us even now. They are hot-tempered, and conceal their dragon-forms with powerful glamours, but I would think with their egos, they'd be pleased to be named an Immortal."

Mark shook his head. "There's something wrong with this dragon. He's... dangerous."

Tristan looked unconvinced. "Many believe gargoyles to be strange and dangerous."

"No," Mark said. "We need to be prepared for a fight here."

Tristan shrugged. "I always am."

They rose from the table and equipped themselves with weapons. As Surcy pulled her daggers from the weapon's chest, her hand recoiled as she brushed against the gun. Her flesh tingled uncomfortably at its nearness. She wasn't sure why most paranormal beings hated the feel of the weapons, but she knew they often malfunctioned when they were around any way.

The demons likely keep it here just in case it's needed.

Closing the chest, she went back out into the main room, where her demons were ready. Mark sat on a chair, his hands pressed against his temple. Another warning sang through her blood, but she pushed it aside. He knew his limits. *Right?*

"Ready?" Tristan asked, and she knew he was aware of her worries.

She nodded.

Mark rose slowly, and they went to Surcy. They all took hands, and she closed her eyes as Mark sent the image to her. It looked like a mountain top in the clouds. It was a place she could have never imagined, but the picture was all she needed to teleport them there. Taking a deep breath, she felt her powers flow around them. A minute later, the four of them stood on the ledge of the mountain.

"Fuck," Daniel muttered, moving back from the edge. "Of course it had to be high up."

Tristan shifted into his gargoyle form, his wings spreading wide behind him as his flesh changed to the stunning color of wet-stone.

She tore her gaze from him and placed a steadying hand on Mark, who looked even paler. "I think this is as close as I could teleport to it."

"Dragons don't like to be disturbed and always create shields around their lairs." Tristan explained slowly. But then, he looked up and frowned. "But unlike the legend, they don't enjoy living in desolate caves. They enjoy wealth and beauty, such as large manors and castles. This seems... unusual."

She glanced up to the cloud-covered top of the mountain. "We had better start climbing if we plan on being there any time soon. And, uh, maybe Tristan should take Mark up, so he can get a good view of the place and see if there is anything else he can tell us about it."

Tristan nodded and wrapped his arms around Mark. It worried her that the druid didn't refuse him. In seconds, Tristan began to flap his large, stone wings and rose above them, disappearing within the clouds.

"No problem, we can climb," Daniel muttered, turning to the almost sheer rock, his eyes travelling slowly up.

Surcy moved beside him, reached up, finding a handhold, and pulled herself up. It wasn't that she enjoyed climbing, but without her wings, she was left with little choice. She hoped Tristan had the sense not to leave Mark alone at the top.

The climb was more of a challenge than she ever

expected. Sweat made her clothes stick uncomfortably to every inch of her body, and she was breathing hard. Several times she nearly lost her grip, but Daniel was always there, one hand clenching the back of her shirt as she gained a stronger handheld.

Glancing up, she saw the top of the mountain just above them and knew her shaking legs would thank her when she got to solid land.

But just as her mouth curled into a smile, a roar shook the earth, sending tiny rocks and dirt raining down onto them. She had to press closer to the rock to keep from falling, even while her heart raced.

"What the fuck was that?" Daniel asked, sounding out of breath.

"I'm guessing an angry dragon."

He said nothing, but neither of them moved for a long minute, as if waiting for a dragon to come bursting toward them. When nothing terrible happened, she took a deep breath and looked above her once more. They needed to get to the top. If Tristan and Mark were facing an angry dragon, they would need all the help they could get.

She reached for the next handheld.

14

Tristan could not take his gaze from the dragon. Gargoyles were not quick to anger. Their decisions were made with intelligence and strategy, not influenced by emotion. But rage consumed him now. This... was wrong.

The dragon had black scales at one point, but now they were nearly gray. Its flesh hung from its grotesquely thin body, and its wings had patchy holes. The chains that bound its neck were thick and covered in spikes, which even now bit into its flesh, sending dark blood running down its scales in rivulets.

His fists clenched. Whoever had done this would die for their cruelty.

The creature was immortal. No matter how it starved. No matter how it bled, it could not die. This was an existence he would not wish on his greatest enemy.

The dragon roared again, but only a puff of smoke left its lips. There was no chance a dragon in this condition could breathe fire.

"That's the Immortal," Mark whispered beside him, leaning against the cave wall.

Tristan nodded. "So, how do we free him?"

Mark shook his head. "I don't know."

Tristan allowed his senses to stretch out. The chains contained a spell that prevented the dragon from shifting and from breaking the chain. The magic was ancient, powerful, and perhaps created by Caine himself.

As he stared at the chain, he realized that there was a good chance he could break it. Gargoyles were good with stone and metal, anything that could be used to create.

"I think I could free it."

"It'd kill you before you could," Mark said, pushing off from the wall. "If we could reason with it—"

"Him," Tristan added, because now he was sure it was a male. "Shifters cannot remain in one form or the other for too long. Being a dragon for so long means that he has almost entirely given into the animal within him. I don't even know if he could understand us now."

"But we can *try*," Mark asserted.

Tristan didn't have a better idea, so he nodded.

Mark cleared his throat and adjusted his glasses. "Uh, hello—"

The dragon roared. He tried several times to climb to his feet, sending bird bones scattering with every movement, but eventually collapsed back down. His head lay on the ground, but his spinning silver eyes never left them. He looked hungry. And desperate.

Mark took a slight step closer. "We're here to help you. We know that you're an Immortal. We know that Caine imprisoned you here, and we can free you, if you'll let us."

The dragon neither moved nor responded. He just watched. And waited.

Mark inched forward.

Tristan looked between the druid and the dragon's chain. "Not too much closer or he'll reach you."

"He can't even get up," Mark said, frowning.

"For a meal, he can."

Mark paled a bit and nodded. "Do you understand us? Can we help you?"

Still, the dragon said nothing.

The druid inched forward, and everything happened at once. The dragon shot toward him, and Tristan yanked him back, far out of the dragon's reach.

He roared, massive teeth snapping. Drool rolling from his mouth as he struggled against the chain, flinging his body over and over toward them.

Tristan patted Mark's shoulder. "He is a beast now and nothing more."

A second later, they heard something behind them.

Surcy gasped. "What have they done to him?"

"The bastards tortured him," Daniel muttered.

"And now he's lost to his primal side," Mark explained, sounding hopeless. "Tristan may be able to break the chains, but we can't get close enough without it killing us."

"So then, let's feed it," Daniel said, as if it was the easiest thing in the world.

They all turned to the fire mage as one.

He shrugged. "The best way to gain an animal's trust is to feed it and show it that you won't hurt it. We won't rescue him quickly, but we can rescue him."

Mark smiled. "You're a freaking genius!"

Their plan was harder said than done. Surcy teleported away and appeared back on the ledge below. Tristan plucked her off of it, brought her back to the dragon's cave, and they threw the dragon whatever meat Surcy had bought. They spent the afternoon doing nothing but feeding the dragon, but even so, it continued to stare at them, waiting for more.

And yet when Tristan moved forward, the creature was always watching, ready to make him his next meal.

They left in the evening and came back each day for seven days. And each day they sensed a change in the dragon. He seemed... less angry. He didn't roar at their approach, and he didn't snap when they got closer.

He wasn't ready yet, but Tristan felt confident that soon he would trust them.

On the seventh day, as they sat at the cave entrance, waiting for the dragon to finish, they heard a strange sound from the back of the cave.

The dragon stiffened and turned slowly, staring into the darkness.

They tensed. Was it Caine's angels? Or something even more dangerous?

And then, three haggard people appeared at the entrance to a small tunnel. The dragon lunged at them, and the people cowered back, but his chain took him nowhere near them.

One of the people, a woman with long, tangled black hair and a dirt-streaked face looked at them in shock. "We thought... we thought we heard voices."

Tristan could not take his eyes off of her. She looked as thin and filthy as the dragon. Was she a prisoner here too?

"We're here to free the dragon," Surcy said, her voice hesitant.

The woman's eyes widened, and she looked between them and the dragon. "You won't survive that."

"We have to try."

For a long minute, tension sung between them. At last,

the woman spoke, "I'm Winter. This is Autumn and Spring. And that dragon," she said, pointing at it, "is Summer. We are the Immortals of the seasons, and Caine has trapped us here longer than we can remember."

More Immortals?

"Is there no other way out?" Surcy asked, although they all already knew the answer.

Winter shook her head. "Only past Summer. And he's no longer himself... just a mindless dragon."

Surcy stood, and they followed her suit. "Well, we're here to save all of you from Caine."

Winter nodded. "I don't think you'll succeed, but you're the first ones to try."

The man named Autumn took a step closer to them. At one point, his long hair was likely the color of fall leaves, but now it was covered in dirt and grime, so much that the color was a muted brown. "We've been surviving on the bugs and rats we find in the tunnels. I'm all for anything that might get us out of this hell. That fucking bastard Caine, leaving us down here like animals, knowing we'll starve but not die."

Mark spoke, his words soft. "I'm so sorry he did that to you. But we have a plan, we're feeding him. We're going to try to calm him enough to remove his chains. And once he can shift, he should regain some of his mind."

Autumn looked at the dragon. "Sure you don't have any dragon tranquilizers?"

Daniel laughed. "If only."

Spring moved forward. Her hair fell down to her ankles, hair that had once been blonde. And her skin was pale. Dead flowers sprouted from her hair, and her expression was that of hopelessness. "You should know there is another reason why we emerged from the tunnels today."

Tristan frowned. *This doesn't sound good.*

"This is the day the angels come. They give us scraps of food and ask us if we have forgotten the outside world yet."

His heart sped up. Angels? If they came, there was evidence everywhere that people had been here. The bones of all the meat they'd been feeding the dragon littered the floor, and the creature no longer looked nearly as starved and crazed.

"If they come, our plan is doomed," Tristan said, low enough so the Immortals wouldn't catch his words.

"But—" Mark began.

"If they do not kill them in fear of us saving them, they will wait here and spring a trap for the next time we come."

"We can't save him today," Surcy said. "He isn't ready. He'll kill you."

Tristan looked between the beast and the Immortals. He had no choice. He couldn't leave them to suffer, not knowing what Caine and his angels would do now that they'd been found. Yes, the dragon still seemed unable to communicate with them, and gave no indication of his human-side, but Tristan would take the risk.

He had to.

"I remove his chains. Today."

"And what if you actually succeed in releasing him, and he immediately eats all of us?" Daniel asked, with a frown.

"All of you will go to safety."

"Like fucking hell," Daniel said, shaking his head.

"I'm made of stone. I can endure some of the dragon's attack."

"Some," Daniel emphasized. "Not all. His teeth will turn you to dust."

Tristan shrugged. "Then, I'll avoid his teeth."

"Surcy, tell him what a dumbass he's being," Daniel

shouted, drawing the gazes of the Immortals and the dragon.

Tristan's gaze swung to her, and their eyes met. For a minute it was hard to breathe. Did his little angel have any idea the effect she had on him? He was certain she didn't have a clue.

She didn't remember their many moments together, or their nights spent tangled in each other's arms, but he did. And it killed him to not be allowed to touch her now.

Curling his hands into fists, he willed himself to look at her without seeing her. To not notice how fluid, how graceful her movements were as she moved toward him. He told himself that her skin wasn't flushed and healthy, that her long, black hair wasn't silky and begging to be touched, and that the curves of her face and full lips weren't flawless.

But even his own mind screamed that he lied.

She was... stunning.

Her breathing increased, and his gaze moved to her breasts. The slight rise and fall of the twin mounds were intoxicating to watch. His body begged him to reach out and stroke them, to cup them in his hard hands and feel their delicious weight.

But he could not touch her. He would not touch her. Not until she loved him again.

"Tristan?" she said his name softly.

Does she feel our connection too?

"Yes."

"Do you really think you can do this?"

He nodded. Of course he could do it. It was dangerous, but he was not easy to kill.

Reaching up, she pushed his hair back from his face, tucking it behind his ear. A thousand memories came back to him in a rush. Of the first time they met. Even as an angel hunting demons, the connection between them had been powerful. Her slightest touch made him feel more than he had in all his years as a gargoyle, and the power that moved between them was there, even now.

Rising up on her tiptoes, she pressed the lightest kiss to his lips.

He held himself still, afraid of what he might do if he let the wall between them crumble.

"You be careful," she whispered. "Do you understand me? Because if you let that dragon hurt you. I'll kick your ass."

He smiled. "You won't be rid of me so easily, little angel."

Her gaze darkened, and she leaned up again. This time when she kissed him it wasn't lightly, and he felt the wall between them falling. His arms wrapped around her, pulling her closer, and his lips slanted over hers. She was so soft, his angel. Her mouth hot and hungry against his. And when she parted her lips, her tongue tangling with his, he forgot all about the dragons and the Immortals.

This was all he wanted. Surcy. In his arms. Safe and loved forever.

When she pulled back, breaking their kiss, they were both breathing hard. He stared at her, wanting to see the familiar face of a lover. Instead, her expression was surprised. Like it was their first kiss. It both hurt and fascinated him.

She might never remember him, but maybe she could love him again.

"So," Mark cleared his throat. "What's the plan?"

Tristan tore his gaze from his love and stared at the tired druid. "You three find a place to hide. When the dragon is released, we do not know what he will do. He may instinctually shift into his human form. He might become crazed and hunt like a starved animal. You do not wish to be his next meal."

"And if he does that, what will you do?" Mark asked, looking as if he disapproved of their plan.

"I will get as far from him as quickly as I can."

Daniel laughed. "I guess that's a plan."

Tristan looked between the two men. One frowning. One smiling. And yet, they were both worried. *Do not be concerned. I won't leave you so easily.*

"Take care of her," he ordered them.

Daniel nodded. "We will."

And there it was. He didn't just mean right now. He meant if anything went wrong. And they both knew it.

He didn't watch them as they slowly left the cave. He might feel something then, and he couldn't waste time with such things now. Instead, he turned his gaze to the Immortals on the other side of the cave.

"I am releasing him now. Stay far enough back that he cannot reach you."

Their eyes widened, but they obeyed him.

Turning to the dragon, they openly evaluated each other. Gargoyles and dragons were typically allies. For all the rumors about dragons' tempers and selfishness, they didn't like powerful beings preying on humans either. There were times in the past the creatures had even fought at his side.

We are the same, he sent the thought to the dragon.

Perhaps it was his imagination, but he thought the beast stiffened.

I am going to free you. And you are not going to kill any of us. You may shift. You may hunt. But we are not your enemies.

The dragon's silver eyes swirled, but he didn't send a thought in return.

Truly, Tristan wasn't certain whether he'd forgotten how to respond, but understood, or if he was completely lost to the beast.

Closing his eyes, he shifted into his gargoyle form. It took only seconds for his flesh to become hard stone, and for his stone wings to sprout from his back. When he was finished, he took a deep breath, opened his eyes, and inched forward.

When he drew close enough for the beast to attack, the dragon remained still, watching.

Tristan hoped that was a good sign as he closed in. The dragon's leg twitched as he drew near his foot, but still, the beast did not attack.

His heart raced as he came to stand just beside his head. This close up, the dragon was even larger. Big enough to close its jaws around him in one deadly bite. Never before had he approached a wild creature this large and this unpredictable. And he hoped never to have to do it again.

I will remove your chains now. It may hurt, but then you'll be free.

To his shock, the dragon turned its head, showing him the chains around its throat.

Dark blood ran from the sharp tips that pressed into its throat from the collar, more flowing with his movement. It turned Tristan's stomach, but he forced himself to focus. The collar was strong and thick, but he sensed the weak points in it. Reaching forward, he wrapped his hands on either side of the weakest point and began to pull.

A low growl emanated from the dragon's chest, but he didn't attack.

Tristan took that as a good sign and continued to pull. A crack formed in the metal. He was breathing hard, pulling with all his might. His stone hands commanded the metal to weaken, to break. He seemed to press a vibration into the material that sent the crack deeper and deeper. Every muscle in his body strained. His teeth clenching painfully together. He was so close.

So close.

But still, the chain held.

The dragon moved slightly. More blood ran from where Tristan was unintentionally digging the spikes deeper into its throat. Soon the beast would become impatient. Soon he would attack.

Tristan could feel his one chance ticking away with each second that passed.

And then, like a crack of lightning, the collar broke, hitting the ground.

The sound seemed to echo around them. Tristan inched back as the dragon rose onto its feet. Rotating its neck, he seemed to be testing whether the collar was truly gone. And then, he threw back his head and roared.

Only this was a sound of triumph.

Tristan smiled. Soon the haggard creature would be powerful once more.

And then, the air changed. Tristan frowned and looked to the cave entrance. What was wrong?

Something hit the ground outside of the cave. The dragon's head whirled to the sound.

And there, in the entrance, angels approached. Three of them, holding dead birds in their hands. One spoke. The other two laughed.

Tristan tried to move back, but he wasn't fast enough. The dragon moved like lightning, knocking him back against the cave wall with a power that made his vision blacken.

The screams of the angels echoed around him, and the

most horrible sound came. Of bones cracking and blood gushing.

Tristan sucked in deep breaths. He knew enough of battle to know what happened. As his vision returned, he struggled to his feet. His chest, back, and head ached, but he was fine. Stumbling to the back cave, he barely entered before spotting the Immortals.

They ran to him.

"Our collars," Spring whispered, pointing to the thin bands of steel.

Steadying himself, he grasped hers and snapped it with a flick of his wrist. She wept happy tears as he moved to Autumn and Winter. When all of their collars hit the ground, Autumn grabbed his shoulder.

"Thank you. The Seasons are in your debt."

"You are not safe yet. Caine will simply catch you once more. There is a sanctuary for your kind. You must go there, until it is time to overthrow him."

Autumn's cracked lips curled into a smile. "Send me the image, demon, and we'll get there."

The Immortal closed his eyes and pressed his forehead against Tristan's. Tristan thought of the paths to the sanctuary, and then of the sanctuary itself. He tried to show it from the ground and sky, seeking to give them as much information as possible.

At last, the Immortal pulled back. "Thank you. That will do."

He nodded, and the three battered Immortals left the cave, backs straight.

There was something wrong. He was certain of it the moment they came out into the dragon's empty space. It wasn't the entrance, which was splattered with blood. It was something in the air that he couldn't quite put his finger on.

Walking out into the open, his jaw dropped.

Dozens of angels surrounded the weakened dragon as it struggled to flap its wings. Their soul-blades were lit with light, and they swung each time he snapped at them. The dragon turned its head, saw him, and roared, only it was a sound of desperation.

A shiver moved through his body, and his hand went to the sword at his back.

"They'll kill him," Summer whispered.

"No, they won't," Tristan told her.

Moving forward, he severed a head from one of the angels. That got the others attention. Two turned to look at him. The dragon clamped its teeth over one of them, and threw back its head, devouring the angel.

Chaos erupted in the white-winged angels, a few raced at him, while the others spread out their circle around the dragon. Tension hung between them as he faced them, hoping they wouldn't notice the helpless Immortals behind him.

One sword struck his. The sound of metal on metal rang through the air.

He pushed back his opponent. Caught the blade of another angel, and kicked it in the stomach, sending the massive man back.

A blade struck his shoulder, vibrating through his stone body.

Fool.

He whirled, catching the angel's shocked expression as he sliced his head off.

More attacked. Blades struck him from every angle. At first only an annoyance, but after a time, the soul-blade sent aches through his body. The damn blades were different than regular ones, imbued with angel magic.

Unfortunately.

Gritting his teeth, he continued to move until the dragon was behind his back. His large wings flapping hopelessly. And then, to Tristan's shock, the beast began to rise into the air.

The angels, damn them, followed the beast as it wobbled in the sky on its broken wings.

Tristan felt fury uncurl within him. Clutching his blade more tightly, he shot into the sky after them. The battle was a dangerous one. The dragon was driven by a need to survive. Tristan had to stay close, had to knock the angels back as they attacked the dragon's wings.

And yet, the angels were everywhere, teleporting into the sky, surrounding them. The sky filled with white-winged bastards hell-bent on destroying an innocent creature.

The dragon let out the most horrible sound, and then, it shifted in midair. A man fell from the sky, his eyes closed, his face pale.

Tristan dove for him, catching the shifter in his arms. His heart raced as he refused to look back at the angels who surrounded them. He just flew with all his might, choosing a direction at random. He could not let the Immortal die. He had to save him. Not because of Caine, or the fight, but because this man was an innocent who had been tortured and destroyed as a person.

Tristan knew what that felt like.

His heartbeat filled his ears. He could sense the angels just behind him. They shouted for him to stop, but an angel couldn't compete with a gargoyle.

Slowly, the noise faded away. He continued to fly without slowing, but he also glanced down at the man in his arms. He was massive, even for a shifter. It was clear from his broad shoulders and the size of his hands that he had once been a muscular man.

His filthy blond hair had grown long, and a straggly beard hung to his belly. Tristan thought of the dragon with its broken wings and its sagging scales.

Looking behind him, he saw the angels far in the distance, still losing ground. Soon, this man would be safe.

But what of Surcy? And Mark? And Daniel? What of the other Immortals?

His instincts screamed to turn back, but it would mean death for the broken shifter in his arms. And so, he kept flying but he never stopped worrying.

15

Surcy crouched beside Daniel and Mark in the small cave hidden just around the corner from the main entrance.

"We have to help him!" Surcy whispered, trying to rise.

Daniel caught her arm and pulled her back down. "Sit down, and shut up. Or you'll make things worse."

Rage uncoiled within her. "Don't tell me to shut up, you shitbag!"

She tried to shake her arm free of him, but his grip only tightened. "I'm not a... shitbag. But they're fighting in the air. We're useless there. We'll be sitting ducks, so you have to use your brain a little."

"My brain—!"

Mark cut her off. "Daniel, don't talk to her like that. But Surcy, he's right. We can't teleport up here. If we want to escape, we have to scale down a mountain... which we'd never survive with the angels attacking, so our best bet is to stay here."

"But—"

Suddenly, Daniel rose slightly, looking behind her out the cave entrance. "Stay here. And I mean it."

And then, he ducked out of the cave.

Surcy's heart clenched. She whirled to follow after him, but this time, Mark caught her arm.

"What are you doing?" she said, feeling panic rise within her. "We need to stop him. You're right. He's exposed out there. It's too dangerous!"

Out of the corner of her eyes, she caught a movement. The three Immortals were hovering by the entrance to the main cave.

Sweat dripped down her back. If just one angel saw them, their lives could end with the flick of their swords. Yes, they'd be reborn... so that Caine could torture them all over again, but that would be the end of their chance to help them.

"What is he doing?" Mark murmured.

Daniel walked past the Immortals. Pointed to where Surcy and Mark were hiding, then kept going. As he emerged out of the shadows of caves, and out into the open beneath the angels. He pulled something from his pocket. Not his sword from his back. Not a dagger. But a small silver item from his pocket.

"What is that?" she asked, heart hammering.

He turned back and gave Mark and Surcy the saddest smile, then flicked his finger. A little flame blossomed to life. And as she watched, the flame spread over his body until he blazed. It continued further until it lit the very sands, spreading out until the entire top of the mountain behind the caves blazed with fire.

Then, and only then, he withdrew his sword.

The angels had seen him. Watching the flames grow in

confusion. And then, they circled above him, staying out of reach of the fire.

Surcy's entire heart squeezed in fear. The three Immortals left the cave entrance and raced to Surcy and Mark. Mark helped them sit down near the back of the small cave. She heard him murmuring words of comfort to them, but her focus was on Daniel.

What had he been thinking? Yes, it was the distraction the Immortals needed to reach them safely, but what would he do now with an army of angels surrounding him?

She doubted he'd thought further than that. The damn fire mage.

And yet, her legs ached with a need to run to him. Seeing him out there, exposed and alone, made her feel helpless. And she hated feeling helpless.

Again.

"How do we help him?" she whispered.

Mark knelt down beside her, wrapping an arm around her shoulders. "He'll be fine."

"Can he last forever like that?"

Mark took a long second to answer. "No, eventually the fire will kill him."

She turned to him in shock.

"But not for a long time," Mark rushed out.

"Then, what's his plan?"

The druid shrugged. "I'm sure he has one."

Surcy pushed his arm off of her. "Why don't you seem worried?"

Mark sighed and moved to rest his back against the side of the cave, suddenly looking very tired. "I'm less worried about this situation and more worried about what's going to happen when we get home. Daniel has a way of getting out of tricky spots, but he's in a bad place. I don't want this to encourage him to start using fire again."

She looked between the angels trying pathetically to use their swords on Daniel, but flying back every time they got too close. "I don't know how you have so much faith that this insane situation is going to work out, but he can't control his addiction."

Mark closed his eyes. "Spoken like a person who knows nothing about addiction. I'm sorry, Surcy, but angels he can fight. Himself? Well, he might not be strong enough. Especially without you at his side."

"I'm on his side," she said, feeling prickly. Hadn't she *just* been talked to by Tristan about this?

In answer, the Immortal known as Spring spoke. "If we could shift, we could help end this. But we can't. It's like our bodies forgot that side of ourselves after so long."

Surcy turned to the blonde, and her emotions changed. The three Immortals looked so weak and so sickly. Their backup plan couldn't be that they'd shift and save them all.

It's our job to protect them.

No, not ours. *Mine.*

Mark was exhausted from using the God Finder. These people were suffering. She was the only one who could help Daniel. But how?

And then, it hit her. A completely insane plan. But one she knew could work.

"What do you think the chances are that the angels will find you here?" she asked.

Spring answered with certainty. "They won't. They'll either assume we already escaped or that we're in the tunnels."

She nodded, feeling more certain with every passing second. "Mark, keep them hidden here. We'll be back."

"Surcy…"

Rising, she slowly and cautiously made her way out of the cave, sliding along the outside of the larger cave until she reached the entrance. Daniel was still surrounded by fire. The angels were no longer attacking, but staying just out of his reach.

Let's do this!

"Daniel!" she shouted.

He turned, his eyes widening in shock.

As one, the angels turned to her too.

"Get rid of the fire!" she shouted, then, taking a deep breath, she ran towards him.

His jaw tensed, and the fire around him suddenly leapt from the earth, latching onto the white-winged angels. Screams surrounded them as their wings burned, and sparks of fire fell down from the sky like rain.

She didn't slow, even when she felt the sting of the embers on her skin. She just continued toward Daniel. His arms were outstretched as he forced all the fire from her path. And from him.

But as he did, he took several steps back, the sand and rocks at the edge of the mountain tumbled over the edge as he neared it. And yet, he seemed unaware of how close he was to falling to his death.

She sped up, her muscles burning as she sought to reach him in time. When she drew closer, his gaze moved back to her. She saw the moment he realized she wasn't going to slow. He put his hands out as if to stop her, but she was going too fast.

Her arms wrapped around him. For an instant, she tried to flap her wings, her instincts going against all logic. And then, they plummeted over the edge, tangled together.

The wind whistled around them. Daniel wrapped

himself around her, as if doing so could protect her from the fall. And when she felt the tingle that told her she'd passed through the barrier surrounding the mountain top, she teleported.

They hit the ground, her on top of Daniel. Their breathing was hard, his strong arms wrapped around her. For a long minute, they just held each other, too relieved to do anything else. Her eyes squeezed shut, and she inhaled his smoky scent. It was familiar, and yet, unexpected.

"What were you thinking?" he whispered. "I had a plan."

What was I thinking? "I needed to keep you safe."

"Why?"

She pulled back and stared at him as his arms dropped to his side. "You have to know I care about you."

The look of absolute pain that ran over his face made her heart stop. He didn't know. He actually didn't know.

"Daniel..."

He shook his head, closing his eyes.

"I care about you. I know things are different now, but—"

"You have absolutely no reason to care about me. I'm an asshole. I don't know how I got you to love me the first time, but you're not going to be that dumb again."

She couldn't breathe as she leaned down and brushed a light kiss against his lips.

His eyes opened, two dark pools of anguish.

"You're not an asshole... you're wings."

"Wings?" he repeated, raising a brow.

"Yes," she felt more certain now. "When wings are curled up, they look like nothing. Maybe even ugly piles of feathers... but when they open up, everything changes. They're beautiful. Not just beautiful, but capable of amazing things! Some people are wings. And you're wings.

There's nothing wrong with the fact that it takes you longer to open up to people. And there's nothing wrong with the fact that that's the time where they see who you really are."

"I'm wings," he said, and the slightest smile touched his lips.

She gave him another gentle kiss. "And wings are absolutely loveable."

Her words seemed to break something inside of him. His arms wrapped around her, pulling her tightly against him. His mouth sought hers, and then, they were kissing. Not their hard normal kisses, but this time it felt different. Less rushed.

When he broke the kiss, they were both breathing hard, staring at each other. And then, his gaze moved away from her and widened.

"Where did you teleport us to?"

She glanced around. They were in a cabin of some kind. There was a mustiness in the air, and the curtains were drawn, but it was still a strangely comforting place, with a tiny kitchen, living room, and a massive bed in the back. They were lying on a rug in front of a dark fireplace.

"I don't know."

His gaze moved back to her. "You don't?"

She shook her head.

He seemed to be choosing his words with care. "This is another hideout we have. A cabin we used to go to when we wanted to be alone."

I've been here before?

Her heart raced. "I don't remember it, but I took us here, so... so I must still have my memories somewhere inside of me!"

He smiled, making her insides tremble.

"What if I could remember? Then everything could go back to the way things were! I could be me again!"

His brows drew together, and his smile vanished. "Listen, I know we've all been walking around like a pack of heartbroken animals, but your lost memories don't mean you're not yourself anymore."

"Daniel, come on."

"I mean it. You're still you. And you have to know that even if your memories do come back, you won't be the same."

Her stomach pitched. "Do you not want me to remember?"

He smirked. "I'm just saying I don't care either way. You're Surcy, no matter what."

The strangest realization hit her in that moment. Daniel meant it. He really didn't care whether she remembered or not.

Wrapping her arms around his neck, she pressed her face against his throat and tried to hold back the tears. She'd felt such pressure since the moment she'd met these demons to remember who she was and to become the woman they loved. The idea that they could love her just the way she was made her feel relieved in a way she could never explain.

"It's okay," he whispered against her head, and his hand went to her temple. Slowly, he began to rub circles into her skin, and she melted with a slight moan. "See, you love it when I do this, now and then."

She relaxed more deeply against him. "How long do you think it'll take for the angels to leave and for us to go back?"

"Maybe we'll check back right before nightfall."

That would probably give the angels enough time to

sniff around, but also time for them to climb down where she could teleport them safely away.

"Do you think Tristan is okay?"

Daniel laughed. "Of course. Tristan can handle himself."

She closed her eyes. It was nice to feel the rumble of Daniel's laugh through his chest. This man was strangely comfortable to lie on. Even though they'd slept together many times before, she'd never felt closer to him than she did in that moment.

"What should we do until then?" she asked, not really caring.

"I have an idea."

She didn't know what to expect at the slight teasing note in his voice, but she never expected what happened. They played cards at the table. A game he assured her they both loved. And as soon as she got the hang of it, it became an absolute blast, because she kicked his ass every time.

Daniel was not a good loser.

She was not a good winner.

So the game was more fun than she ever imagined. He swore. She danced obnoxiously every time she won, and they ate popcorn and drank soda.

When it came time for them to go again, she felt strangely sad. "It was nice to pretend that everything is normal for a little while."

He looked up from where he was still seated at the table, putting the cards away. "One day we'll be able to enjoy things like this all the time. When we've defeated Caine, and we're sure you're safe from him."

"And that his angels can never drag the three of you back to the demon-realm," she added with force.

He smiled. "That too."

Rising, she watched as he moved toward her. His blond

hair was messy after all they'd been through, sticking up in random spots. His face was neatly shaved, as always, showing the incredible lines of his face.

It was hard to breathe as he got closer. Daniel was truly a beautiful man. He didn't have the ruggedness than Tristan had, or the nerdy-hotness that Mark had. He had something else. A confident spirit hiding a softer side. *Like wings.*

He took her hands with a shyness she hadn't expected. "Shall we go?"

She nodded, but didn't teleport them. "Thanks... for the cards."

He smiled, his genuine smile. The one that seemed uncertain. "You're welcome."

But still, she hesitated. "Are you staying away from fire?"

His eyes widened, and she saw it in his face.

"Daniel..."

"I'm working on it."

Her entire chest ached. "You kicked it once. You'll kick it again, because we're here for you. We won't let you fall down that path."

He nodded, but his expression was troubled.

"Is it when you go for walks?"

His gaze met hers again. "Yes."

Her hands tightened on his. "Then, for now on we go for walks together."

He let out a breath that seemed to shake his whole chest. "I'd like that. I've just been so lonely, and—"

She released his hands and shot into his arms. *I'm such a freaking idiot. Of course he's lonely. I've been using him for sex and not caring about him. Tristan was right to scold me. I deserved it!*

"From now on you're not going to be lonely. You're going to be annoyed, because we're going to stick to you like glue."

He laughed, that rumbling laugh she loved. "All right."

When she drew back, she caught his hands again. "Ready?"

"Ready."

Taking a deep breath, she transported them back to the edge just beyond the barrier around the mountaintop, praying the angels were gone. And praying Mark and the Immortals were safe.

16

Mark stood on legs that shook and leaned heavily against the cave wall, wincing and wrapping an arm around his stomach. He didn't want to tell the others, they'd already been through so much, but he felt like he was going to throw up. His entire body felt wrong. Weak. And it scared him.

I need to protect these frightened prisoners. Not lay in a corner puking. Damn it!

The worst part of it all—this was his fault. He'd known he was pushing himself too hard. He just didn't realize he was making himself fucking useless in the process.

Next time he looked for Immortals, he would take more breaks from the God Finder. Because this time he'd plunged forward, every time he saw a glimpse of an Immortal in a vision, and was shot back out of the vision, he pressed back in. He'd done it over and over again for weeks, determined to pull all the pieces together enough to see where to find them.

Because of that feeling.

When his stomach calmed, he peered out of the cave

entrance. The angels seemed to have vanished an hour earlier, but he could never be sure about the slimy little creatures. As weak as he felt, he couldn't risk giving away their hiding place. If they found them, and he was unable to fight, everything they'd done would be for nothing.

And yet, he couldn't escape the nagging feeling he'd had the last few weeks. The one that said their time was drawing to an end. That the battle between the realms would rage soon, and without the Immortals, they'd lose.

He wanted to believe the feeling was nothing more than anxiety, but he knew better. His druid's staff might have been broken, still lying in pieces in the sanctuary, but his powers still lay within him. And they screamed that he needed to keep pushing himself, no matter the price, or all would be lost.

But I won't be useful to them if I can't help.

As the sun set, its rays painting the top of the burnt mountaintop, Surcy and Daniel came over the edge. He moved without thinking, walking out to greet them. Surcy ran into his arms, holding him tightly, and Daniel patted his back, with a smile. He sensed a change within them. They seemed... closer.

It made him happy. When he died, they'd need each other.

"So, what's the plan now?" he asked, forcing the words past his tired lips.

"We take them to the sanctuary," Surcy said, no doubt in her voice. "Do you think they're strong enough to climb down a little?"

I know I'm not.

"No."

She nodded. "Then, I hope they aren't afraid of heights, because I can teleport them after they jump."

"We aren't," Spring emerged from the cave, followed by the other Immortals. "But we can't go to the sanctuary first."

Surcy frowned. "Why?"

"We need to go to our sacred island to regain our strength."

"You'll be exposed to Caine and the angels. They could take you back at any moment."

Spring smiled. "It's the only way we can regain our strength, and we're certain it's where the gargoyle will take Summer."

Surcy looked like she wanted to keep arguing.

But Daniel answered. "Alright, we can take you there, but we need to leave as quickly as possible."

Spring nodded.

Autumn and Winter came to stand at their sides, looking as if they might collapse at any moment.

"Show me where you need me to teleport you," Surcy said, moving toward them. "And I can take you one at a time over the edge."

Autumn stiffened and moved in front of Spring. "You can teleport?" His eyes narrowed. "Are you an angel?"

Surcy paled. "I *was* an angel. I turned my back on Caine."

Instantly tension sang through the air. Mark looked between the Immortals and Surcy.

Uh oh.

17

S urcy stared at the Immortals. They looked... upset. Her stomach churned, and for some reason, she felt ashamed.

I didn't choose to be an angel. They can't possibly hold it against me. Could they?

"I'm no longer serving Caine because I have to; I'm serving a cause I believe in."

"Which explains your missing wings." Spring reached out and touched her back lightly.

Surcy winced and nodded.

Autumn crossed his arms over his chest. "And we're really just supposed to accept that?"

She didn't know what to say. It was almost surreal. She'd lost so much when she lost her wings, and yet, she was still seen as an enemy by these Immortals. Is that how the rest of her life would be? The thought made the weight on her shoulders feel heavier.

"You can always stay here," Daniel said, indicating the mountain. His tone dripping with sarcasm. "I mean, sure we risked our lives to save all of you, but if the fact that she's an angel bothers you that much, stay here. Keep wasting away. Keep starving. Why the fuck should we care?"

Winter held out her hands. "Enough! Apologize, Autumn."

Autumn glared.

"Apologize you angry old, shifter!" Daniel ordered.

Autumn kept glaring, but mumbled out an apology.

Winter nodded. "Sorry, he gets cranky when he doesn't eat. And he's been hungry for a long time."

Surcy tried to push away the hurt his words had brought, but they lingered. *At least you have Daniel here to defend you.* Glancing back at his angry expression made her sadness ease. It was actually kind of nice to see his temper directed at someone else.

A little laugh exploded from her lips.

His gaze jerked to her. "What?"

"Nothing," but she couldn't keep the smile from her face.

Like a force of nature, he came to her, sweeping her hair back from her neck and kissing her until her knees went weak. When he pulled back, she clung to the front of his shirt.

"Wow."

"Maybe that'll teach you not to laugh at me."

Unable to help herself, she slid her hands down his chest. "Or maybe I'll tease you more."

Suddenly, arms wrapped around them. She turned to find Mark grinning like mad. "You two made up!"

"We weren't fighting!" Surcy protested.

Daniel reached out and ruffled Mark's hair. "Yeah, we made up."

Mark kissed Surcy's neck in just the right spot to send tingles through her body. "Good."

"We might want to continue this when everyone is safe," Daniel said, but there was humor in his voice.

"Of course," Mark pulled back and fiddled with his glasses, giving them both a tired smile.

Surcy wanted to pull them both back to her again. She wanted to inhale their familiar scents and feel their strong arms around her. But as always, there wasn't time for that.

Trying not to look disappointed, she turned and walked back to the Immortals, who watched their exchange with interest. When she stopped in front of Spring, she was suddenly struck by the underlying beauty beneath all the dirt. Her eyes were the purest blue, like the petals of an extraordinary flower. No mortal had eyes like hers.

Her heart raced as Spring lifted her hands and touched the sides of her face. Instantly, images bombarded her. There was a beach of glowing golden sand. Large trees with golden apple-like fruits , and houses woven from nature itself were concealed within the trees.

Home. The word echoed through her mind with a sadness that rang through her very soul.

Surcy opened her eyes and nodded. "I'll get you there."

The Immortal smiled. "I know you will."

Surcy stepped back from her and looked at the other Immortals. Autumn no longer watched her with suspicious eyes; instead, his amber-colored eyes were filled with interest. And Winter's eyes, so dark they were black, were oddly intelligent. As if she was evaluating everything that had taken place, and had come to some kind of decision.

"Who should I take first?" she asked, feeling strangely humbled in their presence.

"Spring," Autumn and Winter said at once.

The Immortal took her hand without question, and Surcy nearly jumped at how cold and boney it was. Leading her to the edge of the mountain, she stopped and looked back.

"I'll be right back."

Daniel raised a brow. "We'll be here."

She almost laughed. But instead, she looked at the Immortal. "Ready?"

Spring nodded, and as one, they jumped.

18

I t was long past nightfall when Surcy had finally brought everyone to the tiny island. Tristan and the Immortal were already there when they reached it. The dragon-shifter was in his human-form, but unlike the other Immortals, he never spoke. He just moved among the trees eating apples with a desperation that spoke of his hunger. In fact, all the Immortals ate and ate.

As the night grew later, she began to nod off. All the fighting, along with using her powers, was exhausting. And yet, she couldn't get comfortable on the beach.

I'm pretty sure I have a seashell poking me right in the back. Ugh! She pulled it out, lay down again, and still squirmed, unable to rest.

When Tristan suggested she head home to get some sleep, she gratefully leapt at the chance. If she didn't get a good night's sleep, she had no idea how she'd be able to teleport so many people to the sanctuary in the morning.

And after that, my demons can sleep for days, if they want to.

She returned to their empty home and showered, then changed for bed. A strange tension filled the air, and she found it difficult to sleep. Staring into the darkness, she tried to decide why she was feeling so uneasy, but nothing came to mind.

The Immortals and my demons are safe. I'm safe. So what's wrong with me?

A teasing wind blew the white curtains near her balcony, bringing with it the sweet scents of Daniel's garden. The scent reminded her of the sweet demon. And, at last, she was able to close her eyes. With a smile on her lips, she snuggled deeper into her pillows and felt herself slipping into sleep.

Something made her open her eyes as she shifted. And a man was standing over her.

Her eyes flashed open again. A scream caught in her throat.

Even though she'd never seen him through his cloud of dark magic, she knew it was him. Caine. He radiated a power so intense that it took her breath away. His hair was dark. His eyes pale and cruel. His body was neither thin, nor muscular. Instead, he was built like a man whose strength was woven into every inch of his flesh. He wore a simple dark shirt and pants, and his expression was intense.

"Surcy," he practically purred her name.

On instinct she tried to teleport away, but his powers held her there.

"What are you doing here?" she whispered, in horror.

He slid closer. "Must we do this every time?"

Her hands were sweaty, clutching the blanket to her chest as if it could stop whatever was about to happen. "I don't understand."

He slid even closer. "You, Surcy, are my spy. That is the only reason I didn't simply call you to me and throw you into the Soul Destroyer. And now, you and your filthy demons have angered me by taking my Immortals. So, you are going to show me where they are, and I'm going to end their worthless lives."

No! She stiffened. *She would not allow this to happen. She couldn't!*

"Don't touch me!"

He lifted his hand. "Always so stubborn. Even until the end."

Taking a deep breath, she watched as his hand grew closer. Then, moving faster than she ever had before, she called her soul-blade to her and struck out. His hand went flying.

She leapt on the bed as a scream of pain left his lips, then jumped toward him, determined to sever his damn head. Instead, he raised his good hand, and she hung in midair for a painful second before being thrown back against the mattress.

Her soul-blade vanished, and then he was over her, his one good hand wrapped around her throat. "You're going to pay for that, Surcy. And your demons are going to pay for that. I might not be able to kill them yet, but I can make them suffer, and I will."

She struggled, thrashing on the bed. Her legs kicking wildly, but his hold on her throat was relentless. Her vision dimmed, and then she felt him, like a spider crawling through her mind. She fought him, with every ounce of her being, but she knew the second he found what he was searching for. The location of the four Immortals.

His voice held immense power. "I knew they wouldn't just go to the sanctuary."

She felt tears slide down her cheeks.

"Now, where did you hide that damn mermaid?"

Again, he pilfered through her thoughts, her memories,

with a reckless, violating power that made her choke down a sob.

"Ah! She too refused the sanctuary." She felt his cold lips press against her temple. "I wonder how it will feel to know that every risk you took, everything you and your demons did was for nothing. I will simply take the Immortals back, and leave you all to suffer the consequences."

"Bastard," she ground out, more tears rolling down her cheeks.

She felt his lips smile against her skin. "You know what the best part is? You're the one who betrayed them. You ruined it all for them." Then, his voice grew quieter. "And you won't even remember it."

That horrible feeling came again, of him prying inside her mind, and then, everything went black.

19

Tristan watched as the morning sun rose over the horizon, feeling strangely satisfied. This island was one blessed by the four Immortals who controlled the seasons. No one else had ever walked these golden sands, until them. He could feel the healing energy of the powerful magic coursing through his skin. He liked the impact it had on those he protected.

The Immortals had eaten the golden apples for hours. And over that time, they'd visibly changed. Their skin glowed. They gained weight, filling out their bodies. And they seemed to hum with power with each passing second.

They'd then stripped off their clothes and bathed in the waters that surrounded the island. Waters that sparkled like stars. When they'd finally emerged, they wore clothing representative of their seasons. And they also wore smiles.

Only the Immortal known as Summer seemed to have no emotion. He ate, bathed, and curled up on the sands without a word or a sign of his feelings. And yet, when they slept, they all slept curled together on the sands.

We were right to take them here.

He'd debated whether he was making a mistake. The shifter he carried had woken, pointing and guiding Tristan as he flew him. Tristan had thought he should bring the shifter to sanctuary, but seeing how their lands healed them, he was glad he didn't. They needed this.

They deserved it after all they had been through.

And now, Daniel and Mark were sleeping contently near him, the Immortals only a few feet further away, and Surcy safely in their home.

He felt... happy. Nothing made him happier than when the people under his protection were safe. Perhaps it was the gargoyle in him, but he didn't mind.

Closing his eyes, he felt the sun as it caressed his flesh. Since meeting Surcy, he found himself staying in this form more and more. He no longer wanted to hide in stone. In fact, he felt like an entirely new person. All the years before he'd been broken, he slept unless his village needed him. Now, he couldn't imagine hiding in his stone form.

It felt... nice to be alive.

Something sliced through his chest, and pain shot through every nerve in his body. His eyes opened, and Frink stood over him, grinning. The angel pulled back his soul-blade and blood poured from Tristan's mouth. He tried to shout, to warn the others, but it came out gargled through his blood.

Frink's smiled widened, and he plunged his sword into Tristan's chest again, pinning him back against the sand. His head turned. White-winged angels crept along the golden sands, their blades drawn, as they surrounded Mark, Daniel, and the Immortals.

Drawing every ounce of strength within him, he spit blood, and shouted, "angels!"

The word wasn't loud. But it was enough. Daniel and

Mark shot awake. The angels raised their soul-blades, and suddenly, swords appeared in the demons' hands. Metal clashed with metal, and then they were leaping to their feet.

The Immortals rose too, their expressions giving nothing away as the angels surrounded them.

He couldn't let them die! He couldn't!

Frink grabbed his face and pulled him to face him as he leaned down on his sword, twisting it more painfully inside him. "I can't kill you, demon-scum, but I've been told I can make you very, very miserable."

Tristan spit blood in his face, then coughed up more.

Frink wiped it away, his eyes wild.

And then, Daniel severed the angel's head from behind. The fire mage stood over him, pulled the blade out of his chest, then turned to face the next attack.

Tristan willed his flesh to turn to stone. It took longer than usual, but with the blade gone, it was possible. He knew the instant it worked, because the pain echoed through him, but was no longer unbearable.

Breathing hard, he still couldn't rise. But his thoughts began to clear.

A roar shook the air.

Letting his head drop to the side, he was shocked to see the dragon he'd rescued. He'd transformed again, but this time he no longer looked as sickly. Still too thin, but his scales were a brilliant gold, and his wings looked stronger.

The angels scattered back from him.

He lashed out at them, and the angels scattered into the air. Summer rose into the air, following them like a being focused only on revenge. On the shore, Spring shifted. Where the woman once stood, a silver dragon rose. Without slowing, she followed Summer into the sky.

Winter shifted into a black dragon. A massive creature

with dark eyes. And Autumn changed beside her, into a red dragon. They too launched into the air.

The angels Mark and Daniel fought were plucked off the ground. Thrown, ripped into pieces, and torn with vicious teeth. Tristan had seen many battles in his lifetimes and had seen a lot of blood, but this was different. These dragons were out for blood. They didn't just want to kill the angels, or win the fight. They wanted to make the angels suffer.

Screams filled the air. And with each second that passed, Tristan fought to rise. He didn't know what he would do, but he was determined this would not be the first battle he didn't fight in.

When he managed to climb to his feet on unsteady legs, he looked down at Frink. How many times had they killed the damn angel? He was growing tired of killing him.

In the air, the dragons circled the sky, roaring fire. No angels remained, but still, the dragons circled. Their flight changing slowly from one of rage to one of pleasure.

When Daniel and Mark moved and took his arms, placing them over their shoulders, he relaxed between them. They watched the dragons with an unspoken amazement. They were beautiful creatures. It was rare to see one. The beings were powerful enough to create glamours that even demons couldn't see through.

And there was something amazing about seeing them free. Never, in all his days, would he forget the sight of the broken dragon, of its dull scales and broken wings.

Beauty like that should never be destroyed so thoughtlessly.

At last, the dragons landed lightly on the shore. Within seconds, they transformed. For the first time, the four Immortals truly looked like powerful beings of legend.

Magic surrounded them and lit them from the inside out, like a glow.

Summer moved forward. His broad shoulders and muscles humming with strength. "Thank you."

Daniel responded. "You're welcome."

After a quiet moment, Mark spoke. "You know we sought you out because we intend to overthrow Caine."

Summer nodded. "Because he controls your angel."

Tristan stiffened. "He does not."

Summer's silver eyes focused on him. "He does. He could call her back at any time. Make it so painful that she has no choice but to return. But he doesn't, because she's his spy."

Tristan pushed away from the demons who held him. "No! She would never!"

The shifter tilted his head. "She does not have a choice. None of us had a choice. Caine plays with our minds. Our memories. He plucks what he wishes from her, and erases her memories of what he has done."

He felt sick, so sick he thought he might hurl right on the beach. "That can't be true."

Spring moved forward, the bright, lively flowers in her long, golden hair, moving slightly. "It's true. Her life is in his hands as long as he sits upon the throne in Zedussa. When we are restored to power, the angels will be under our control once more."

"I can't believe it," Mark murmured softly.

Summer looked sad. "How do you think the angels found us? Don't forgot this."

The massive shifter moved toward the water and Shifted back into the golden dragon, before gracefully leaping into the sky.

Spring followed him, but paused at the water's edge. "We will not forget what you've done for us."

When she transformed, and Autumn followed her, only Winter remained.

The woman was stunning. Long black hair framed a pale face that was overwhelmed by two dark eyes. "You might love her, but you cannot trust her. Even though it is against her will. Do you understand?"

Tristan nodded, numbly.

Winter turned to look at the sky. "We will go to this sanctuary of yours, until it's time. But you should also know, none of us believe you will be able to save the others. The odds are simply... against you."

She shifted, and then the dragons circled overhead several times before shooting off into the sky.

"Do you think they're right?" Daniel whispered.

Tristan was surprised when Mark answered. "The angels took me because of the God Finder. I couldn't figure out how they found out about it, but if they can pull information out of Surcy..."

Tristan collapsed onto his knees. The bodies of the angels turned to light and disappeared, leaving behind golden sands covered in blood. And yet, none of that mattered, because now they knew the truth. Surcy was not safe. Surcy was not free.

And Surcy could no longer help them in their search for the Immortals. Yet, if she wasn't useful to Caine anymore, what would he do to her then?

They heard a sound behind them.

Surcy's voice came, soft and shocked. "What happened?"

How can we possibly tell her?

20

Surcy sat at the dining room table with her demons. They'd barely spoken since returning, just enough to say they'd been attacked by angels, and that the Immortals had returned to the sanctuary. A tension she didn't understand hung in the air, and no matter how she tried, it remained.

Even Mark wouldn't look at her.

They ate their spaghetti and salad in silence.

"How are you feeling?" she asked Tristan, turning to the stoic gargoyle.

Instead of answering, he set his fork down, rose from the table, and left.

What happened? How do I fix this?

"Is he okay?" she asked the other two.

Mark said nothing.

Daniel took another bite of his food. "None of us are."

"But none of you will tell me a thing," she pressed, sounding frustrated.

"We need to discuss it first... without you."

She felt her brows rise. "Without me? Why?"

He shrugged. "That's just how it is."

Suddenly, she couldn't take it anymore. She tossed her napkin on the table and rose. "Fine. I'm going out for a little while."

Neither man said anything, so spinning on her heels, she marched to the door. Looking back, she glared at them. "Do you have any idea how crappy it feels to feel like the three men I love are hiding something from me?"

Both turned to stare at her, but she didn't wait for their response, she slammed the door instead. Rushing down the pathway through the garden, she felt her anger grasping her like rough hands. But as the autumn winds swept over her, teasing her hair, she calmed slightly. Going to the little door on the wall that led out into the city, she pushed it open and slipped out onto the sidewalk.

Shoving her hands into her pockets, she didn't look at the people she passed. She felt... lost. Maybe it was because their strange behavior came after the Immortal who didn't want to trust her for being an angel, but she was angry. Maybe she didn't have her memory. Maybe she was *still kind of* an angel. But she was also Surcy, the woman they'd fought so hard to prove she could trust them, to get her to love them.

Freezing in the street, she stared across a little park squeezed in-between buildings. Multicolored leaves drifted from the trees, their orange and red leaves beautiful as they drifted in the wind. But her mind seemed to be frozen on them. Frozen on a thought.

Did she say she loved her demons?

Her heart squeezed. She did!

Searching her feeling, her hands slid out of her pockets. She did love them. Each of them.

She wasn't sure how it happened, or when it happened,

but it had. Suddenly she couldn't imagine a life without them, and that had a significance that made her legs feel weak.

Waiting until a car passed, she sprinted across the street until she reached the park and sat down. She loved demons! She no longer had wings. She still didn't remember being human, or her time with the demons before, but she somehow felt that the time she did have with them was enough.

If she never remembered anything else... she might be okay.

She thought of their mission and about rescuing the Immortals. There were still three remaining, somewhere out there. Once they rescued them, they could overthrow Caine. Yes, there would be a war between the realms like nothing that had been seen before, but after that, the world would be the way it was always meant to be.

Even though she was a wingless angel, she would be part of the force that changes everything.

She smiled and stood. She didn't know what the hell was going on with her demons, but they'd been through a lot. She could put aside her hurt feelings and fix things between them.

And she knew exactly how to do it.

Rushing home, she ignored the fact that Mark and Daniel stopped talking at the table when she walked past. She went to her room and took a long shower, scrubbing every inch of her body. When she was done, she looked in her mirror. She didn't have makeup, or a hair dryer, so she brushed her hair until it didn't look like a wet dog, and then went to her closet.

There was nothing sexy. Not. One. Single. Thing.

But she saw one of Tristan's simple white shirts and put

it on. Going back to the mirror, she felt a wave of nervousness. The shirt was see-through. It might be too much... but then, she was going for sexy. They'd find this sexy, right? Taking a deep breath, she went to her bed and slid between the sheets. Lying down, she stared at the ceiling. Did she just, call them? How exactly did a woman coax three sexy men into bed with her?

She kind of wished she could just make them start things.

Curling her hands around the covers, she gritted her teeth. Nope, she could be brave. She could show them that she loved them and wanted to be with them. And that she didn't care if things were strained between them, she just wanted them.

She cleared her throat. Then, said nothing.

I feel stupid.

Climbing out of bed, she stood in the center of the room, still uncertain what to do. *Calling, "come sex me up, boys," sounds wrong, somehow.*

She stared hopelessly at her open door, striving for something that didn't make her sound like an idiot.

But to her relief, she didn't have to say a thing. The three men suddenly appeared at her door, Mark knocking awkwardly on the frame of the door. When his gaze rose and landed on her, it widened, then slid over her.

"Come in," she said, her voice no louder than a whisper.

They entered. There was tension in their shoulders, even in their expressions, but when they saw her, the air changed.

A shiver went through her body. Daniel was staring at her as if she truly wore nothing at all. His gaze moved to her breasts, where she knew her nipples were clearly visible, then down to the junction between her thighs. Mark, on the other hand, looked like he'd been smacked. His mouth hung slightly open, and his gaze was fixed on her body.

Tristan stood frozen. His hands curled into fists. "Surcy —" His deep voice was a groan of warning.

"I want you. All of you," she said, forcing the words past her lips.

He started to shake his head, "I told you—"

"I love you."

His face seemed to pale.

"It hit me today, that I do. And that I don't care about anything else. I just want all of you."

He crossed the room and touched her cheek, his fingers feather light. For a minute he seemed lost for words and she hung on the air, waiting. Finally, he cleared his throat. "We need to talk to you first."

Willing herself to be bold, she stood up on her tiptoes and pulled him down into a kiss. Instantly, he melted against her, his lips desperate. When their kiss finally broke, she reached for his shirt and began to pull it up, revealing his mouthwatering stomach. Her fingers instantly brushed the muscles, glorying in the fact that she got to touch them, loving the way her body heated up as she stroked his flesh.

He caught her wrists, breathing hard, eyes closed. "We need to talk first."

She shook her head. "No. It can wait."

When he opened his mouth, she let her hands slide down to the button on his jeans. Flicking it open, she drew down the zipper, then pulled off his pants. His words died, and his eyes popped open as she knelt down and slid his boxers down.

And she stared. And stared.

It was like she was seeing him for the first time. So big, so hard, and all hers.

Running her finger slowly along the length of him, she was satisfied when his cock jerked.

"Surcy," her name was ripped from his lips, the sound of a man being tortured.

Continuing her light exploration of him, her gaze was glued to the precum that shone at his tip. Unable to help herself, she leaned forward and licked him.

He groaned, his entire body spasming.

If he likes that...

Parting her lips, she took him inside of her hot mouth. The gargoyle shuddered, and his hands went lightly to the back of her hair. As she slid him in and out, Tristan bucked into her mouth, a man trying desperately to keep his control.

But she wanted to make him lose all control. She wanted to reward him for his patience with her and show him just how much he meant to her.

She cupped his balls, squeezing them softly, as she sucked harder and harder.

His movements became more rushed, wilder, but she knew the moment he snapped.

He roared, a sound that was all demon. His hands dug into the back of her hair, and he began to thrust into her mouth as if he owned her. Each time his cock hit the back of her throat, she gagged around him, but didn't stop. She wanted to taste him when he released. She wanted to know she'd been the one to make him lose control.

When her name tore from his lips, and a shudder went through his body, he exploded. She continued to suck him as he fucked her mouth wildly. Until he slowed. Until he stopped, holding her hair lightly, keeping himself inside of her.

Looking up slowly, she met his hooded gaze.

"I love you," he said, drawing himself out of her.

She felt herself tremble and her nipples harden. "I love you too."

When Mark and Daniel moved to her sides, Mark helped her rise. Daniel's warm hands caught the bottom of her shirt and drew it up, letting his knuckles drag against her exposed flesh. It made goose bumps erupt over her skin. It made her clench her teeth to keep her moan inside.

At last she stood before them, naked, and yet, it didn't feel strange at all. It felt... right. Instead of being exposed, she was being freed.

Mark let his hand slide lightly over her back, circling around the scars. Instead of the reminder bringing her to tears, she felt... okay. If she had her wings, she couldn't have her demons.

She'd trade her wings for her demons any day.

His lips followed the tail of his hands, pressing light kisses on her shoulders, then her back, and then cautiously, onto her scars.

It was like her soul smiled. Maybe the angels hated her. Maybe other beings might not accept her. But her demons always would.

Tristan made a small sound of contentment and lay back on the bed. He watched them with hooded eyes, his gaze never leaving their actions. Daniel moved closer, kissing her softly, his hands resting on her hips.

She moved without thinking, unbuttoning his shirt and pulling it off his broad shoulders. For a second she was overwhelmed by him. He was so good-looking. So impossibly beautiful.

Her hands slid down the hard muscles of his chest, past his stomach, and began to work the button on his pants. Daniel moved closer.

"You know what you're in for, sweetheart?"

She didn't look up at him as she nodded and yanked his pants down.

His boxers and pants came off as one, and then she was left staring at his proud erection.

"I've seen you naked before," she said, hating the husky quality to her words.

He leaned closer and nipped her ear, causing her breath to rush out. "I mean, are you ready to have three big dicks in you?"

She shuddered. "Yes."

"Good," he bit her ear again. "Because I can't wait to sink into that glorious asshole of yours again."

She felt her cheeks heat and her nipples tighten.

"Now, undress Mark."

He spun her around.

With shaking hands, she undressed her demon. He watched her every move as she undid the buttons on his shirt and slid the material off his broad, delicious shoulders. He shuddered when she trailed her lips across his throat as she took off his pants, sinking to her knees to remove them.

And when she rose, she wasn't surprised when Mark pulled her into his arms, lifting her off the ground. Her legs wrapped around his back, and his cock sat hard between them. Reaching down with one hand, she took him in her grip and used his length to slowly slide against. She didn't let him enter her, just rubbed herself back and forth along him, feeling herself grow wetter with each stroke.

When he cursed, she almost smiled, if it weren't for the heat uncurling in her belly.

Instead, she pressed his tip at her entrance and took him deeper and deeper into her tight channel. Her breathing hitched as her body squeezed around him, and when she reached his hilt, she dropped his length and wrapped her arms around his neck, breathing hard.

When Daniel grasped her breasts from behind, she moaned. His fingers teased her nipples, and he moved closer until he was firmly pressed against her... until she was practically sitting on his cock. Then, he reached one hand down and steered his length—in and out of her juices.

The word fuck became a chant behind him as he continued to coat himself, and then, he withdrew, growing silent. Holding her breath, she clamped her teeth together, waiting. But she didn't have to wait long.

Like a familiar lover, he spread her ass from behind and eased himself into her. With each inch, her body squeezed him in protest, but he took his time, teasing her nipple with his free hand each time she stiffened.

Mark didn't move inside her, but he pressed like kisses along her neck and shoulder, murmuring words of love that she didn't quite understand, yet felt.

When both men were inside her, she sat between them, breathing hard, shocked by the strange sensation. She'd never felt so full. So surrounded. It was—

And then they moved.

"Damn it!" Her nails dug into Mark's shoulder, and she felt her eyes widen in shock.

Every nerve was alive, screaming in pleasure. She couldn't catch her breath. She couldn't draw in a single thought. They continued to move, sliding in and out with slow, careful movements.

She didn't know what to do, her back bent. She moaned, thrashing her head. How was it possible to feel like this? To feel so good that she wanted to crawl out of her skin, or perhaps stay in it forever, she wasn't sure which.

Her core grew hotter, tightening like a cord. The men

started to move faster. She sensed their control slipping as they didn't just slide back into her, they pounded into her.

To her shock, she began to move against them, rocking in tune to their thrusts. The men groaned in pleasure, and she rode them harder, loving the sounds of their arousal. Loving the feeling of being filled by them.

When she felt a spark burst into light within her, she reached for it, moving faster and faster. Her orgasm struck her like something wild and dangerous, she tossed her head back screaming, grasping her breasts and pinching her nipples as they held her, claiming every inch of her.

The world swam away. Time ceased to exist. Everything inside her was alight with something she'd never imagined before.

And then, the two demons exploded into her, their groans of pleasure hoarse. Their bodies shuddering around her.

When their thrusting finally slowed, she collapsed between them. They kissed her neck, slowly, almost drunkenly. And their grip around her tightened.

"That was... incredible," she whispered lamely.

She felt Daniel smile against her neck. "That was nothing. We've only just begun."

Her head swam as Mark pulled out of her, but Daniel stayed buried inside of her, grasping her thighs to keep her from falling. He carried her across the room and laid her directly onto Tristan.

Her eyes widened as he spread her legs, and his cock eased into her wet channel.

"Already?" she whispered in disbelief.

As if in answer, he began to thrust inside of her. Daniel grunted, and his cock swelled in her ass. And again, two powerful demons were riding her.

For one minute it was too much, she'd just orgasmed. Her nerves were still screaming in pleasure! And then, to her shock, a moan slipped from her lips. She felt it again. The tingles running through her body. The goose bumps erupted on her flesh.

"Fuck me," she groaned.

Tristan nipped her ear. "With pleasure, my angel."

When her orgasm hit again, she sobbed. It felt too damned good. Like something she'd always wanted. Like everything inside of her had wanted nothing but these demons all her life.

Her head felt light. Her muscles tensed, and the demons exploded inside of her once more.

They rode her like wild men for several long seconds before Daniel collapsed on top of her from behind.

They lay like that breathing for a long time before Mark joined them on the bed, lying on his side. She opened her eyes and looked at him. He was already asleep.

Daniel pulled out of her from behind and lay on her other side. He mumbled something she was sure she didn't want to hear, then fell asleep too.

When Daniel gently stroked her ass, her eyes began to close.

"Next time, I'm going to slap this delicious ass."

A smile touched her lips. *I hope so.*

21

Mark slipped out of the bed they shared and looked back at Daniel, Tristan, and Surcy. His heart raced. *This is it.* The God Finder hung heavy around his neck, pulsing with power. It had a vision for him. And the power it swelled with this time was overwhelming. He'd have to funnel a lot of his life-force into it to unlock the image and hold onto it.

Perhaps more than I have left.

Like a parasite it took from him. It didn't take just his druid magic or just his demon strength. It took everything within him, everything that made his body work.

I'm not going to survive much longer.

The thought made his throat close. His fate was sealed. He knew that from the moment he began his search for the Immortals, but it was always his destiny.

Surcy, Daniel, and Tristan were my reward. My great loves.

The Fate's words echoed through his mind, even after all this time. There had been times when he was a boy, alone and afraid in the world that he'd felt the Fate had made a mistake. That she'd chosen the wrong person.

And when he died, he'd thought that was the end, that he had failed the realms.

But now, he knew. Everything had happened just the way it was supposed to.

Soon he would die again, but he'd have fulfilled his destiny this time.

Looking at Surcy, Daniel, and Tristan again, he memorized their faces and then, slipped from the room and walked on bare feet into the living room. An instinct that crawled along his spine made him grab a pad of paper and pen off the countertop. Gathering a blanket around his naked body, he tucked it around his waist and lay down on the soft rug before the quiet fireplace, the paper and pen beside him.

His entire body trembled, but he refused to acknowledge how frightened he was. How much he worried that tonight would be his last night on earth. *Because no matter what the vision takes from me, I shouldn't die right away. I still have too much left to do.*

The thought comforted him enough to calm his racing heart. To make him reach up. Closing his eyes, he placed one hand around The God Finder.

What do you have to show me now?

Immediately, he felt the power of the newest vision in a way he never had before. It drained the life-force from him like a dying vampire, drinking and drinking until his eyes rolled back in his head.

The images came faster than ever before, and for once, began to pull into a vision more quickly than he ever imagined. Angels surrounded three people. No, not people, the Immortals. The angels flashed their swords, and the people fell to their knees.

"Caine has given up trying to take your powers," Frink

said, his voice harsh.

"Powers?" a woman said, "I don't know what you're talking about."

Frink's gaze narrowed. With a flick of his wrist, her head fell from her body. "Now, we're done with games. Your souls will be eternally destroyed, and no one will stop Caine."

The people began to wail as the angels closed in, and the sounds of their screaming rang in his ears.

Eyes flashing open, his heart hammered in his chest. The Immortals weren't dead yet. It was a vision of what would soon pass.

They had to rescue them. Now.

Or else I don't think we'll be able to save them. We'll fail.

He knew where they would be kept once they were caught. The vision was clear. Zedussa. The angel realm. The place Caine ruled from. A formidable structure meant to protect the Immortal Ten. And one he doubted they could reach.

So we need to find them before my vision can come to pass.

He had no idea how they would save them in time. But they didn't have a choice.

The Fate had been clear. Without all ten of the Immortals, they'd fail.

And if the last of the unfound Immortals are taken to Zedussa before we can save them, our time is up. We'll have to wage the war here and now if we have any hope of saving them before Caine can destroy their souls.

Which means we'll also have to take the Immortals out of hiding, and have them fight at our sides, whether they're ready or not. Because without them, we can't take on the entire angel army and Caine himself.

If they lost, there would never be another chance again.

Rolling to his side, too weak to rise, he grasped the pen

and began to scribble on the paper. Once he was done, he flopped back on his back. Everything inside him felt wrong. Tired. As if even his heart was beating more slowly.

As blood ran down Mark's nose, and his vision wavered, he wrapped his hand more tightly around The God Finder.

Show me where they are now.

The power that flowed through him was excruciating, and, he swore, he heard the Fate whisper, *I'm sorry,* as he choked on a scream.

22

When Surcy rose, stretching happily in bed, she glanced to her sides to find Tristan and Daniel sleeping peacefully. She smiled. This was true happiness.

And yet, where was Mark?

Frowning, she slipped out between them and padded out the door. Checking Mark's room, her unease increased. Hurrying down the hall, she stepped out into the main room, and her gaze instantly went to Mark.

He was lying on the floor. A paper lying beside him.

Blood dotted the white material and the rug.

She moved slowly, as if caught by quicksand, and knelt at his side. Touching his chest, she realized it neither rose nor fell.

Heart hammering, she reached for his pulse. There was nothing.

"Mark?" she whispered.

He didn't react.

"Mark!" she shook his shoulders, reality setting in like a punch to the gut. "Mark! Mark! Wake up! Wake up!"

Tristan and Daniel came racing into the room, then were at her side. They all touched Mark. Daniel started CPR. And Tristan pulled her back as she struggled against him.

She watched in horror as they tried to save her love. Her demon. The man who always made her laugh. *My Mark.*

And she held her breath waiting. He had to live. He had to! This couldn't be it!

After an impossibly long time, Daniel stopped doing CPR. He sat back on his heels, staring at the druid, his eyes filled with unshed tears. Everyone looked down at the pale druid speckled in blood. It was as if the air was sucked from the room.

He was dead

Her Mark.

Dead.

Her gaze went to the papers. Maybe... maybe he had left some kind of clue. Some way for them to bring him back!

She grasped the paper and wiped at her tears, staring down as the words came together.

CAINE IS ROUNDING up the final three Immortals. He intends to execute them and destroy their souls. I've written down their current locations. You have to go to them, now. Even knowing that you can't save them all before Caine reaches them.

But you have to try.

And when you've done all you can, you need to bring all the Immortals to Zedussa. You need to wage the war there, before he can kill the Immortals.

And this is the most important part... you can't slow down to mourn me. I knew what I was doing. This how it was always meant to be. If you waste a single second, my death may be for nothing.

. . .

SHE LOWERED THE PAPER, pressing her knuckles to her mouth as she sobbed.

Daniel plucked the message from her, and read it with Tristan at his side.

She knew the moment they were done. Daniel crumpled the paper into a ball and threw it, standing. His anger like lightning.

"Fuck! Fuck! Fuck! You insane, little druid! You didn't have to die! You didn't have to do any of this!"

"Daniel—" Tristan began, his words overwhelmed with sorrow.

"No!" Daniel turned and started to walk away, then stopped. "This is utter bullshit, and I won't hear it. We're not going to go after the stupid Immortals. We're going to march back into the demon realm and pull him out screaming!"

"And then what? Lose Surcy next?"

Daniel froze.

"If we do not stop Caine, all of this will be for nothing, as Mark said."

Daniel clenched his fists. "We can't just leave him dead."

Tristan rose like a stature, powerful and strong. "If we don't act quickly enough, Caine may decide to destroy his soul."

Everything inside of Surcy tensed. That's right, Caine would see his soul in death. Caine would decide what happened to him.

"We need to go," she said, wiping tears from her eyes.

Daniel seemed unable to function, to even move.

But Tristan went to him, placing a hand on his shoulder. "We're going to dress. We're going to get our weapons, and then, we're going to get our revenge."

Surcy nodded. Revenge. That's exactly what they needed. And the best kind of revenge? They'd knock that fucking Caine right off his stolen throne.

And then, we're coming for you, you reckless druid. And once you're safely with us again, I'm going to kick your ass.

But even as the thought gave her strength, her gaze went to Mark's body.

WANT to read the next exciting book in this series? Then grab your copy of Lover's Wrath.

We're coming for you, my love.

ALSO BY LACEY CARTER ANDERSEN

Monsters and Gargoyles

Medusa's Destiny *audiobook*

Keto's Tale

Celaeno's Fate

Cerberus Unleashed

Lamia's Blood

Shade's Secret

Hecate's Spell

Shorts: Their Own Sanctuary

Shorts: Their Miracle Pregnancy

Dark Supernaturals

Marked Immortals

Wicked Reform School/House of Berserkers

Untamed: Wicked Reform School

Unknown: House of Berserkers

Royal Fae Academy

Revere (A Short Prequel)

Ravage

Ruin

Reign

Her Demon Lovers

Secret Monsters

Unchained Magic

Dark Powers

An Angel and Her Demons

Supernatural Lies

Immortal Truths

Lover's Wrath

Legends Unleashed

Don't Say My Name

Don't Cross My Path

Don't Touch My Men

The Firehouse Feline

Feline the Heat

Feline the Flames

Feline the Burn

Feline the Pressure

God Fire Reform School

Magic for Dummies

Myths for Half-Wits

Mayhem for Suckers

Alternative Futures

Nightmare Hunter *audiobook*

Deadly Dreams *audiobook*

Mortal Flames

Twisted Prophecies

Box Set: Alien Mischief

The Icelius Reverse Harem

Her Alien Abductors

Her Alien Barbarians

Her Alien Mates

Collection: Her Alien Romance

Steamy Tales of Warriors and Rebels

Gladiators

The Dragon Shifters' Last Hope

Claimed by Her Harem

Treasured by Her Harem

Collection: Magic in her Harem

Harem of the Shifter Queen

Sultry Fire

Sinful Ice

Saucy Mist

Collection: Power in her Kiss

Standalones

Worthy (A Villainously Romantic Retelling)

Beauty with a Bite

Shifters and Alphas

Collections

Monsters, Gods, Witches, Oh My!

Wings, Horns, and Shifters

ABOUT THE AUTHOR

Lacey Carter Andersen loves reading, writing, and drinking excessive amounts of coffee. She spends her days taking care of her husband, three kids, and three cats. But at night, everything changes! Her imagination runs wild with strong-willed characters, unique worlds, and exciting plots that she enthusiastically puts into stories.

Lacey has dozens of tales: science fiction romances, paranormal romances, short romances, reverse harem romances, and more. So, please feel free to dive into any of her worlds; she loves to have the company!

And you're welcome to reach out to her; she really enjoys hearing from her readers.

You can find her at:

Email: laceycarterandersen@gmail.com

Mailing List:

https://www.subscribepage.com/laceycarterandersen

Website: https://laceycarterandersen.net/

Facebook Page:

https://www.facebook.com/authorlaceycarterandersen

Printed in Great Britain
by Amazon